D0271652

Her eyes directly on him hit harder than the reflection. Five years hadn't aged him so much as refined him. Not a trace of boyishness remained in his face. Preston had his man-face and, heaven help her, it was glorious. Broad. Cut jaw. Cheeks darkened with stubble despite being freshly shaved.

He didn't even blink when he saw her, but the pale blue eyes that had always mesmerized her looked tired. And cold. And every inch as devastating as they had always been.

"Hardin."

His mouth firmed and black brows drew together—more a look of resolve than the scowl she'd expected.

"I was hoping to put off running into you, but we might as well get it over with." He stepped through the door.

"You're meeting me," Dasha blurted out. "Our head is on hiatus. I'm acting head."

"Am I here on *your* recommendation?"

He might not be angry, but he certainly wasn't happy either. Not forgiven—not that she expected to be. She had done nothing to deserve it. Yet.

"Dr. Saunders recommended you to the board." At her request. She left that part out.

"You're who I'll be working with if I stick around now?"

He kept eye contact, and it was all Dasha could do not to look away.

"Yes."

After work she was *so* going to need to spend some time with Ben & Jerry. And maybe Jack Daniel's too.

Dear Reader

One of the most romantic and beautiful places I've ever been is the Opryland Hotel in Nashville, Tennessee. Between the conservatories, the miles of opulent corridors with low lighting, the nightly dazzling fountain shows and the *Gone-with-the-Wind*-like staircase, it's one of the best places to go if you want to actually get to know the person you're with. Romantic and massive, it still manages to provide a feeling of seclusion...and an abundance of little private places to steal a kiss.

And it's never more magical than during the autumn, when every corner is lit up and decorated for the holiday season. When I decided where Dasha and Preston would reside, the *when* was a no-brainer. I'm happy to share a little bit of this place I love, and if you ever get the chance...visit Opryland in the fall.

Amalie

UNCOVERING HER SECRETS

BY
AMALIE BERLIN

Published in Great Britain 2014
by Mills & Boon, an imprint of Harlequin (UK) Limited,
Large Print edition 2014
Eton House, 18-24 Paradise Road,
Richmond, Surrey, TW9 1SR

ISBN: 978-0-263-23900-3

Harlequin (UK) Limited's policy is to use papers that are natural, renewable and recyclable products and made from wood grown in sustainable forests. The logging and manufacturing processes conform to the legal environmental regulations of the country of origin.

Printed and bound in Great Britain
by CPI Antony Rowe, Chippenham, Wiltshire

There's never been a day when there haven't been stories in **Amalie Berlin**'s head. When she was a child they were called daydreams, and she was supposed to stop having them and pay attention. Now when someone interrupts her daydreams to ask, 'What are you doing?' she delights in answering, 'I'm working!'

Amalie lives in Southern Ohio with her family and a passel of critters. When *not* working, she reads, watches movies, geeks out over documentaries, and randomly decides to learn antiquated skills. In case of zombie apocalypse she'll still have bread, lacy underthings, granulated sugar, and always something new to read.

Also by Amalie Berlin:

CRAVING HER ROUGH DIAMOND DOC

These books are also available in eBook format from www.millsandboon.co.uk

DEDICATION

To Suzanne Clarke, for seeing something sparkly and worth polishing in my writing, and for all her wonderful advice, patience and assistance with breaking away the rest of the lumpy coal bits.

To the best critique partners
and writing pals a girl can have:
The Ginger Ninja (Michelle Smart),
The Sassy Scot (Aimée Duffy),
and—as I write this—
The Lovely Birthday Girl (Catherine Coles).

And finally to my husband, for his love and support, for always challenging me and keeping me on my toes, and for proving how sexy a sense of humour can be in a man. :)

Praise for
Amalie Berlin:

'A sexy, sensual, romantic, heart-warming and purely emotional romantic bliss-filled read. I very much look forward to this author's next book, and being transported to a world of pure romance brilliance!'

—*Goodreads.com* on
CRAVING HER ROUGH DIAMOND DOC

CHAPTER ONE

How could a woman be so afraid of a situation of her own making?

Dr. Dasha Hardin stood before the bank of windows in her temporary office, waiting, eyes fixed on the parking lot where she expected Dr. Preston Monroe would park. She did her best to ignore the lump of lead in her belly that had been oatmeal an hour ago. Being the instigator of this meeting didn't mean she had any control over what was to come, and if he put even half the effort into sabotaging her career as he had done his own, she might as well clean out her locker now. The man couldn't control his mouth, and if he told what he knew about her past…

When the lead shifted and wobbled around her insides, she gave up her vigil for the physical embodiment of her biggest regret. Waiting for him, watching out windows for someone to come was too gut-wrenchingly familiar. She'd spent too much of her life waiting on someone to come, lost too many hours. This one would come. Probably.

She prowled away from the window and set about tidying the already immaculate space. If he had found out his morning meeting was with her—that she was the acting head of surgery for St. Vincent's—he might not show up. That was a nice thought.

Fleetingly.

If he came now, that was the better option, otherwise she'd just have to chase him down. She had to try and fix this. She'd promised Marjorie.

She uncrossed her arms and shook her hands out. When had she gone back to the window? Jeez. Calm down, exercise a little self-control. If he came she had to keep the situation civil and professional, and that couldn't happen if her emotions ran amok.

This was her hospital. Everyone loved and respected her. They wouldn't stop her just because Preston hated her.

Even if he told them what she'd done.

Probably.

A light knock came at the door, more of a warning that it was opening than a request. She caught his reflection in the window. The oatmeal-lead flipped over, but it took her a couple seconds to make her body turn around.

No matter how she tried to will herself to be calm, her heart continued to square dance against her sternum.

Her eyes directly on him hit harder than the reflection. Five years hadn't aged him so much as refined him. Not a trace of boyishness remained in his face. Preston had his man face and, heaven help her, it was glorious. Broad. Cut jaw. Cheeks darkened with stubble despite being freshly shaved.

He didn't even blink when he saw her, but the pale blue eyes that had always mesmerized her looked tired. And cold. And every inch as devastating as they had always been. Having no apparent reaction made it seem like he wasn't angry at least, even though he focused on her with a strength that left her feeling skewered.

"Hardin." His mouth firmed and black brows drew together, more a look of resolve than the scowl she'd expected. "I was hoping to put off running into you, but we might as well get it over with." He stepped through the door.

Did he show anger before detonating these days? A brilliant surgeon he may be, but mercurial. His moods had always been a crapshoot, even before she'd painted a blood-red target on her back.

She should speak. The speech. She'd had a speech prepared, back before fear had eaten it.

"You're meeting me," Dasha blurted out. "Our head is on hiatus. I'm Acting Head."

"The lady in HR managed to bypass that bit of information." Preston took his time closing the door and finding somewhere to stand and fill up the whole room.

"I was afraid you wouldn't come if you knew. Don't blame her. My fault." Dasha licked her lips, mouth dry as a winter wind.

"Am I here on your recommendation?" One of his eyes twitched. Should she read something into that? Like the arms folding over his chest weren't enough body language to clue her into his mind-set. He might not be angry, but he certainly wasn't happy either. Not forgiven, not that she expected to be. She had done nothing to deserve it. Yet.

"Dr. Saunders recommended you to the board." At her request. She left that part out. "But he did it from home. His wife is ill."

"When will he return?" He uncrossed his arms.

Good sign? Bad sign? She had to stop trying to read him. This was business. Business spawned by personal mistakes and regrets but still business. Messy business, and she much preferred tidy. "I expect it will be a couple of months." She had to take another breath to force the remaining words out. "Marjorie's in hospice care and he doesn't want to leave her side. But he's expecting your call, if you want to put off coming to St. Vincent's until his return."

"You're who I'll be working with if I stick around now?"

He kept eye contact, and it was all Dasha could do not to look away.

"Yes." After work, she was so going to need to spend some time with Ben & Jerry. And maybe Jack Daniels too. She could make some kind of boozy ice-cream cocktail. Get one of those beer helmets to hold her booze-a-thon and wear out her treadmill. She needed to move. She used up her daily capacity for refined immobility while in surgery; outside the OR sleep was the only other thing that kept her fairly still.

He didn't say anything.

She drummed her fingers against her thigh and waited, holding his gaze. Silence wasn't her favorite, but the longer he went without erupting into a full verbal assault, the easier it got to be around him.

He was still Preston. He was still inherently good at heart, even if he tended toward selfishness. Not that she could say anything about that. Old Dasha was like that too. Much more than New-and-Improved Dasha.

New-and-Improved Dasha had spent time on her people skills and increased her frustration tolerance. She waited until it seemed like he was also waiting on her to say something else. "If you'd prefer to wait until Dr. Saunders returns, you can work directly with him on his cases, but the board wants you working with a surgeon on staff for a probationary period before they decide to finalize the privileges."

"Probation?" he repeated, his voice rising ever so slightly. Okay, yeah, the meeting was wearing on him too. Maybe she should have worked up to that bit.

Preston had never responded well to limits. He plowed his way through obstacles, something that had attracted her to him back in school. That had been the start. Sometimes she wondered if she'd have made it through medical school and residency without that rivalry—even after it had grown into a relationship, the rivalry had still been there.

Preston's idea of support had usually involved him taunting and teasing her until she felt driven to do just as well as she knew he would do. Sometimes Dasha had been certain she'd only pulled it off out of spite. And that crippling need to prove she was as good as everyone else. Worthy of his challenges. Worthy of his friendship…

She sucked in a deep breath. Getting through this meeting meant avoiding those sorts of detours into their past, or at least the emotions that had driven her. She had to stay on point.

As she'd stormed ahead when she should have trod lightly, she did her best now, under the weight of his stare to at least soften the blow. "This is not about your surgical ability. You're brilliant with a scalpel and I don't think anyone would ever deny that, but your people skills are the worst."

"I've never betrayed a friend," he drawled, no longer dancing around the past. "So, between the two of us, I'd say my people skills were superior."

Keeping this completely businesslike and gentle just wasn't going to work—he'd just demoted her from ex-girlfriend to ex-friend. Too much tension hung between them to avoid all the unpleasantness that had come before—all the unpleasantness she'd caused—but she still wanted to try. "Be that as it may, you have a reputation for being difficult. Which I'm certain you know."

"No, I don't know. Explain it, Hardin. I'm difficult?" There it was. Anger. Dampened, kept from burning hot right now, but still present.

God, those eyes. Ice-blue they may be but she could swear there were tiny flames dancing in his pupils. Never mind what that tone… "I'm trying to be tactful, Preston."

"Yes, I can see that. One thing I always appreciated about you was your directness. Spit it out."

"Fine. Everyone expects you to be an ass." Dasha stuffed her hands into her pockets. New-and-Improved Dasha didn't do that because cultured people didn't do that. It was an old habit. Old Dasha did this. She yanked her hands back out and forced them to relax at her sides. "St. Vincent's has a close-knit community. The board likes it that way, the department heads make certain everyone works and plays well together. Staff, administration and physicians, we're all people and, no matter what, conflict needs to be handled civilly." God help her if he brought up how badly she'd worked and played with him. Dasha plowed forward like the thought never occurred to her.

"The board wants good reports about good behavior—that means you can't just speak your mind. Other people can, but other people aren't as sharp-tongued as you are. You cannot pick fights with people. And if you have it in you after all those long exhausting hours of not fighting with anyone, maybe you could work a few of the miracle procedures that makes the board willing to take the risk."

"Why are you willing?" Those eyes followed her every movement.

Willing might be overstating that. "Dr. Saunders and I are both willing to—"

"That's not what I asked," Preston cut in. "I get why he's willing. Why are you willing? What does it get you?"

A clean conscience? Cleaner…

The peace of knowing she'd righted a terrible mistake? Or tried to…

There was no gently working up to subjects with this man. He stormed ahead, setting the pace and expecting everyone else to keep up. And he really didn't seem inclined to back off the subject now. She might as well do it quickly and cleanly.

Maybe it would even salve his pride to know that she didn't view this situation as doing him a favor. "I owe you."

His gaze narrowed slightly.

Dasha waited for him to say something, but when that failed to happen she added, "And you're an amazing surgeon, Dr. Monroe. You would be an asset to St. Vincent's."

He shifted, still quiet but mulling things over, if she had even the tiniest ability to read him anymore.

The fact that there was no immediate refusal didn't really help her endure the silence. She looked down, away from his eyes—like that would give him some privacy to think—and got distracted by the shape of his body. Lean and broad. He filled out the blue scrubs like he was meant to sell them. Dasha had never found scrubs flattering, but there was something equalizing about everyone having to wear shapeless, wretched clothes that did nothing good for most figures.

Until it came to Preston.

He looked good. Narrow hips. Long legs. Broad shoulders. Lean. A swimmer's build. But he was a runner. Like her—and yet another way they'd been rivals. In the class. At the track. During residency. Her libido had been shut down for years, and five minutes with this man and she was undressing him in her mind.

Before he had a chance to answer, the phone in her pocket buzzed and she fished it out to look.

“Big accident on I-40.” She looked him in the eye then. The man had worn scrubs to an interview, he’d come ready to work—or he had before he’d realized with whom he’d be working. As nice and easy as she’d wanted to play this, there was a chance he’d say no if she just asked him to come along. The only way Dasha knew how to make Preston do what she wanted? Make it a competition…dare him. “I’ve been summoned to Trauma One. I see that you came prepared to work, but I know that having to work with me might be too much for you to handle. I don’t want to make you do anything you just aren’t able to do, but do you think you could give us a hand? Maybe it will help you decide whether you want to stick around.”

The way his eyes narrowed made her worry that she’d played the wrong card.

“I know what you’re doing,” he said, his voice level enough to raise warning bells. “Do it again and I’m gone. I don’t really care what you think.

If it didn't sound like you needed help, I wouldn't help. Maybe you can learn something from me."

Before she could say anything, he was out the door and heading in the direction of Emergency. A quick lock of the door and Dasha ran to keep up with his easy jog.

Of course he knew where he was going. He probably memorized the layout of all the buildings before coming. And she was already lagging behind. But that was okay. No, it was better than okay. He would help. They'd need his help today.

And she knew one more thing now: he still looked on her as a rival, otherwise he wouldn't have had to have the last word. And he really wouldn't have thrown down the proverbial gauntlet.

Maybe he wasn't so different after all. She could work with this Preston.

Probably.

A tractor trailer had turned over, crushing some cars and causing others to pile up, bringing to the ER the kind of injuries Preston expected. Until he saw two people pinned together by a length of steel rod. "What was the semi hauling?" He dragged on gloves and followed Dasha to the unlucky couple.

She called orders as a nurse helped her into a gown and gloves.

The grim looks he saw on the staff's faces couldn't be because he was there… Something was wrong. Something besides the carnage.

"You're looking at it," a nurse said, nodding to the skewer. "They were in the car together and had to be cut out."

X-rays hung on the light board, side by side. The woman had a pierced lung, but she was conscious, with fluid currently draining. The man had abdominal trauma. Possibly pierced through his liver. Unconscious.

"Who's on call for Cardiac?" Dasha asked.

"Stevens," someone answered, then added, "But he was in the accident."

The cardiac surgeon had been involved in the tractor trailer wreck?

"Is he injured?" Dasha never stopped moving but her dismay showed for a second before the wall came up. Preston checked the wound on the unconscious man and listened to his breathing then moved to repeat the check on the woman.

"He didn't make it." The same nurse who had answered him.

"Who's on call?" Dasha moved past it, asking

questions of different people, compiling the information she needed to see this through.

If the whole staff were as close as Dasha claimed, he could understand the grimness.

A faint burning started in his left eye. Not tears. Tears would be better. It was the other thing. A warning his eyes were acting up. The last thing he needed, an attack on his first day. Possible first day. If he stayed. It was starting to feel like some psychosomatic self-sabotage. But the job was the best part of him, even his subconscious had to realize that.

It was stress.

He should've been more prepared to see her. He'd known it would happen. He just hadn't expected it to happen first thing.

He also hadn't expected her to be so different. Long hair, blonde in that multicolored way he didn't entirely get… Clean-faced. Put together. But the long hair looked good on her. Thick and straight. Sleek. Polished. Shockingly polished. She was trying so hard to be tactful. It was like speaking to a Dasha twin but wondering the whole time if he'd been *Parent Trap*ped. Was this really the good twin, or was it the tomboy with scraped knees dressed up in her sister's haircut and clothing?

That probably qualified as stressful. Left him a little off kilter.

On her way back to the female patient, Dasha stopped to press her upper arm against that of a nurse, just long enough to break her stride. A touch to comfort…albeit a strange one to keep her gloves clean, but a kind gesture anyway.

A second later she was with the female patient, said a few soft words to her, then straightened and resumed directing. "Dr. Monroe, you're with me. Everyone, we need to wheel these two into the OR. We'll separate them there." The nurse she'd touched looked misty-eyed but jumped in to help. They all worked seamlessly as a team. Not just people working together.

Not once had he had that. Not since residency. He'd forgotten how she could do that…make people want to be their best. Strange contradiction in her character.

Think about it later. Time to work. Preston would never wish this kind of accident on anyone, but submersing himself in work was exactly what he needed.

A group surrounded the gurneys. Pounding feet

and squeaky wheels announced transit of the unlucky couple through the hospital to the freight elevator—the only one big enough to take the gurneys in the position the steel rebar had locked the couple into—then to the large operating room.

"Dr. Monroe, you've got Mr. Andrews." Dasha didn't look at him as she spoke but kept an eye on her patient.

He'd like Mrs. Andrews. In truth, that was probably a two-surgeon job, but they only had so many hands. Maybe he could help Mr. Andrews and then give Dasha a hand, if Mrs. Andrews survived that long. Lots of blood vessels in the area that could be damaged.

They settled in the large operating suite. Neither patient was conscious now. Blood loss did that.

Dasha handed him the surgical saw. "Would you?"

Deferring to him? Okay, that was surprising. He always loved the saw—had almost gone orthopedics because of it. Did she remember that?

Later. Focus. Figuring out her motivations would drive him insane, and now was not the time. She was just another surgeon in a dicey situation with him.

The sound of metal on metal bounced off every

hard flat surface, roaring at near-deafening levels while the steel teeth chewed through the rod.

As soon as it had cut through, Dasha's team pulled Mrs. Andrews's table over, locked the wheels and got to work.

Preston handed the saw to his surgical tech, had his gown and gloves changed, and cut in, following the rod through so much shredded flesh.

As he got to work, the burning in his eye subsided. Maybe he was off the hook. Maybe work really would save him. He and Mr. Andrews would save each other.

"Talk to me," Dasha called, though she needn't have lifted her voice. Back to back, they weren't close enough to touch but Preston could swear he felt her. The air vibrated between them. Or maybe they were touching somehow. Her gown? His? Just something else he needed to ignore.

"Liver pierced. Most of it shredded. There's enough intact to salvage. Working on the bleeding now." Of which there was a large amount. "Yours?"

"Working on the bleeding," she echoed, but in her voice there was a sound he could still identify. She didn't think Mrs. Andrews was going to make it. But if he knew nothing else about Dasha, he knew she didn't like to lose.

"I need to know if they got hold of Nettle," Dasha said, her words rushed, agitated.

But she wasn't talking to him. Let her deal with the rest of department. His focus was in front of him.

How much worse would this morning have been if he and Dasha had had nothing to do but sit around and reminisce? Remember that time when we were dating, and you broke my heart and left me handcuffed to the bed while you stole my fellowship? How much trouble would his mouth have gotten him into then? It certainly would've taxed this new leaf he struggled to turn over.

His mouth had caused him years of trouble, and was the reason he had to work with the woman he'd spent the past decade quasi-stalking.

The best way to avoid Dasha? To know where she was. Know where she worked. Know what conferences she attended. Know where she lived, where she likely shopped, dined and visited. Avoidance of that level required intelligence.

It wasn't really stalking. It was more like anti-stalking. In a stalker sort of way.

And now she stood behind him, no more than a yard away.

Another hour passed.

"How's it going over there?" She asked for updates regularly but hadn't made any more attempts to manipulate him by riling him. Something else he should put off thinking about until later when he was deciding whether to come back to St. Vincent's.

"Closing," Preston answered. "Transfused two pints of blood." No doubt this wasn't exactly what the board had in mind for supervised practice.

"Good. I need you." To help with the surgery. She needed his assistance with the surgery. The words she'd chosen were bad, but they had no hidden meaning.

"How is she doing on blood?" he asked.

A surgical nurse helped him out of his gown and gloves and into a fresh set.

"Up to three, probably adding another..." She never looked away from her patient.

His first view inside the woman's chest nearly robbed him of breath. "We could do with a cardiac surgeon." Could they ever. But in the small cavity his hands joined hers, and they worked in tandem to repair damage that appeared irreversible.

"That's who I've been asking for updates on," she muttered, but she still worked. She wouldn't give up. It was one thing he could give her credit for. Well, that and her skill. On a professional level Dasha was good. It was as a human being that she had failed.

His left eye twitched. He squinted. Sometimes taking charge of those muscles helped. Sometimes it didn't. Working with Dasha might be a deal-breaker. He'd have to think about it.

Later.

When he relaxed the muscles around his eye, his sight sharpened and he saw it. There was a small cut on Mrs. Andrews's heart, but it had not gone through. "Damn."

"What is it?" Dasha stopped what she was doing long enough to look where his hands were.

"She needs to go on the pump," Preston said. "Now." That the heart wall had held this long was a miracle.

"Get the line in her. Go femoral, we don't need any more holes north of the belt," Dasha said, then went back to what she was doing. Already the techs were getting the heart-lung machine in place. They'd started moving the second he said the word *pump.* Preston could get used to that.

A cannula landed in his hand and he prodded around on the woman's thigh to find the artery, swabbed with alcohol and threaded it in. By the time he was ready for the return line, the nurse was waiting for him.

He'd no more gotten it settled than a man pushed into the OR.

Nettle. Preston recognized him then. The name hadn't rung any bells but he'd met this cardiac surgeon before. A golfing buddy of his father's. Which was all Preston needed to know about him. He could jump to some conclusions on his own. Probably decent at his job, but arrogant, and proud of that arrogance.

"Dr. Hardin, step back, please," Nettle said, allowing a nurse to help with the gloves.

"She's got a laceration that isn't through the muscle." Preston gestured to the area where the rod had scuffed up Mrs. Andrews's heart.

"I see it," Nettle said.

Preston stayed put but lifted his hands free and out of the way, ready to go back in if needed. Yes, he wanted the cardiac surgeon to get there, but now he just felt uneasy and over the years he'd learned to trust that feeling. No way was he leaving without a fight, he just had to try and handle it…tactfully.

Dasha talked the surgeon through what had been done, her team continuing with the pump to get the blood cooling so they could stop her heart and repair it. She hit all the pertinent details, which should've made him feel better about the hand-off. But a report wasn't the same as having seen where the rod had been.

"Thank you both. I've got it from here," Nettle said.

"Don't you need another set of—?" Preston almost got through his question.

"I have another set of hands. I brought them." Just then the door swung open and a younger version of the man made his way to the table.

"I'd still like to stay and help." Preston tried to keep his request in a moderate, reasonable tone. Surely the man couldn't object to that. "I'll stay out of the way unless you need me."

"If she needs her appendix removed, you'll be the first person we call," Nettle said. His tone light, no aggression there, but it reeked of condescension.

Nettle had obviously not gotten Dasha's memo on being nice to everyone.

Preston caught Dasha shaking her head almost

imperceptibly at him. Not the time to fight. He knew that. Of course it wasn't the time, but there was no other time to make a stand and stay with the patient. He couldn't just leave now and ask later over drinks.

"She's in good hands," Dasha said diplomatically, and began trying to steer him toward the door.

"You can't be all right with this," he hissed in her ear.

"No," she whispered back, "but it isn't going to help Mrs. Andrews if we distract him." She surreptitiously nodded to a camera above the table.

Preston pulled off his gloves and gown and headed for the door. As soon as she was through it, he grabbed her by the elbow. "Where is the monitor?"

"Next door." Dasha fished her keys out of her pocket again, and before a minute passed they were crowded around a monitor, following the surgery.

"Is this recording?" Preston asked, looking the room over. "Can we zoom in or something?"

"I don't know, and I don't know." Dasha didn't look away from the screen, but she did get the phone and managed to dial while they watched. "It should be fine. He's got excellent stats and qualifications. He's a good surgeon. A little territorial… and it was weird of him to kick us out. Do you two know one another? It seemed like he knew you and didn't like you."

"I noticed." He kept his eyes on the screen. It'd be easier to see if he was there—and easier to pay attention if Dasha was anywhere else—but Mrs. Andrews was her patient too and he wasn't going to be Nettle-like and kick her out just because her proximity bothered him. He was tough. He could handle it. He'd had five years to get her out of his system. This was just like taking a recovering alcoholic to a bar…the temptation was there, no matter how much he knew it was a bad idea to even think about it. Ignore her scent. Don't think about the way she tasted. Don't think about her at all.

If he paid attention to the small screen, to everything the surgeons were doing, he could see if they were in trouble, and—he prayed—have time to get there. Not that it was likely they'd not be able to handle whatever situation they got into, but he just didn't want to let go. The idea that Mr. Andrews would have to recover from surgery and from losing his wife was too much to stomach on his first day. Especially with all this Dasha business he had to stomach.

"You didn't answer my question." Dasha spoke, interfering with his plan to ignore her.

"We've met. Nothing happened. But he golfs with my father. I imagine Nettle hears a lot of ranting from Davis P.," Preston muttered, forcing it to the back of his mind now that he had to try and see clearly from the angle of the camera and the small screen he was viewing on.

"Mr. Andrews is awake." She passed the phone to him, letting him get an update on his other patient.

"Tell him she's still in surgery." He paused and then added, "And with really good surgeons."

God, he hated lying. The man might be a good surgeon—that was still up for debate—but he was an ass. And all this talking interrupted his monitoring. He hung up and refocused. Someone had to make sure it was done right.

Dasha kept one eye on the screen and the other on Preston. Alone in a small room together…at least they reeked of surgical soap, nothing sexy about that.

Despite a near hiccup with Nettle, Preston was a professional in surgery. Somewhere in the back of her mind Dasha had known he would be, even if she'd irritated him just moments before. He took his work seriously. He took his patients and his duty to them seriously. Which was what made the situation at Davidson West, his last hospital, so confusing.

Something had to have happened. Something she needed details about. The missing details worried her.

Fainting during surgery could be disastrous. If he'd simply been ill, the spell had been nothing to dismiss him over. If he'd been drinking, there would've been criminal charges filed. It really couldn't be something bad. Accidental. Not his fault. Had to be.

Or could it have been bad judgment? Something that made him so serious about keeping an eagle eye on Nettle? A bad call didn't necessarily equate with something criminal…

And then there was the strong possibility that he'd simply made too many enemies among the board members and they'd been looking for a reason to get rid of him. Any reason. A man didn't go through five hospitals in as many years without there being a problem.

Whatever it was, she had to find out before they went into another OR. Then later she could focus on finding a way to curb his tendency to shout loud angry words at people who irritated him. And probably it would be smart to be easy with him. Well, as easy as she could be while keeping him in line.

"What did—?" Dasha stopped as Preston leaped up and bolted from the room. "Where are you going?"

"He's closing," Preston said over his shoulder, stepping into the scrub room and grabbing a mask to put over his face.

Dasha followed. "Good?"

"No. Not good. There's a nicked vessel I was repairing. I had to stop to start the pump then he ordered us out. I didn't get it totally finished." He barreled through the scrub room.

"Are you saying—? Dammit!" She fumbled for a mask and followed him through the swinging doors.

"You're not done, Dr. Nettle," Preston said, shaking his head as he entered.

She should be glad he was still using titles. It was a nod toward him trying diplomacy first. A good sign.

"I am," Nettle stated.

"You missed a small bleeder," Preston said, his posture aggressive even if he spoke levelly.

"I assure you I didn't. Leave my OR."

"If you close right now she…will…die." Preston enunciated every word, his hackles rising higher every time he was blown off.

"Dr. Hardin." Nettle addressed her instead. "Get him out of my OR."

She laid a hand on his arm. Preston shrugged it off and gave her such a withering look he convinced her he was right. The temporary position came with a certain amount of authority she was expected to use to settle disagreements like this. "Dr. Nettle, please take one more look." Request. Diplomatic. She hoped.

"Is your ego really so big that you can't even look where I saw it?" Preston added. He could suck all the diplomacy out of any suggestion. "If you let her die because you're too big an asshole to listen, I will file the malpractice complaint myself."

Threats. Great. Although his words came nowhere near violence, it still managed to sound like he planned to kick Nettle's butt if he didn't listen.

And Dasha would have to say something to him about that later. But right now she had to back him up.

Nettle sighed. "Where do you think you saw it?"

"Switch to the other side of the table." The side Preston had been on earlier. "You probably can't see it from where you are." To his credit, he didn't approach the table, merely directed from several paces away. Very precise instructions: where to look; when to move tissue aside.

"I'll be damned." Nettle frowned. "It appears you were right, Dr. Monroe." He set about repairing the damage.

"It happens on occasion," Preston mumbled, still cloaked in anger and clearly with no intention of leaving until Nettle had finished and Mrs. Andrews was safe.

Dasha stayed too. This temporary position interfered with her new paradigm: avoid confrontation. Staying out of fights made it more likely that she could keep Old Dasha at bay. Old Dasha was a little too much like Preston. But if she could change, so could he. In theory.

Preston might lack people skills but he wasn't wrong. And it was unlikely there would be any complaints filed against Preston. Mrs. Andrews wasn't out of danger by any stretch, but there was one fewer vulture circling because Preston hadn't backed down.

She just needed him to figure out some other way besides verbal attack to secure that kind of cooperation. He needed a new paradigm too.

Like yesterday.

CHAPTER TWO

IN PRESTON'S MIND, St. Vincent's had always represented a strange contradictory utopia. The idealized dream job. The hospital where he should've always been, rather than the sentences he'd endured under the thumb of Davis P.

But it was also the thing that had cost him the only woman—no, the only person—he'd ever really felt accepted by. Felt motivated by. Maybe he'd been wrong all this time. Maybe there had been nothing special between them, no chemistry or affection. Maybe she was just that way with everyone.

If he hadn't been all that special to her, it lessened her betrayal. Sort of.

And that thought didn't help at all.

He stood in the men's room, where he'd taken sanctuary after Mrs. Andrews's chest had been closed, and focused on the eye currently threatening to spasm. He could feel it lurking in the tightening muscle.

Stepping to the side, he grabbed some paper towels and wet them so he could apply them to his infuriating left eye.

He couldn't have been wrong about their friendship. Impossible. And he really couldn't have been wrong about the sexual relationship. No one could fake the passion they'd shared.

And thinking about sex and Dasha was also a bad idea.

He wrung out the towel and wet it again.

This morning, the offer from the head of surgery at St. Vincent's had felt like a reprieve. A stay of execution. He wouldn't have to call in his father for favors—which was how it had been seeming. He'd never done it before, and the idea of starting now stuck in his throat. The fact that he'd even considered it galled him, let alone the idea of volunteering to suffer one of Davis P. Monroe's epic lectures.

The only other option was starting over in a new town, far from the man's shadow.

Now it just seemed like he was swapping one evil for another. And this evil, while undoubtedly better looking, couldn't be trusted to have his best interests at heart. He wasn't even sure he believed her claim that she'd arranged this because she owed him.

His eye twitched open beneath the wet towel then refused to close. He dropped the towel in the sink and focused. The eye had opened so wide it looked surprised.

Scratch that. He didn't look surprised in one eye. He looked like Popeye.

He could definitely add stress to his triggers.

As if sensing a moment of weakness, his phone in his thigh pocket started to vibrate.

Preston fished it out and looked at the screen. Davis P. No way. He sent it to voice mail.

He couldn't stomach a lecture right now. And, really, he didn't see that he'd be able to suffer one and hold his tongue for the rest of the day. Not when he was questioning his past, his future…hell, even his value as a surgeon, as a man.

Better text something.

Just like that, the decision was made.

Can't talk. At work. Took position at St. Vincent's.

Home. He'd go home, give the injection in his left eye—the biggest offender. He'd been hoping to treat the problem with medication, the kind he could take with water. But another attack this soon made it injection time. Maybe switching to the botulin injection would be enough to counter the stress he expected Dasha to stir up.

Sixty days. He could handle two months to be at the hospital he'd always wanted. He just had to tread lightly around Dasha. Not get too close. Forget what had happened. Forget the feelings.

And when his probation was over, he could go back to forgetting her.

Mid-afternoon on any given Middle Tennessee October day closely resembled summer. Hot during the day but cold at night.

Dasha hated October, and had since she was a child. Her father had left in an October. Her mother had died in an October. And now Marjorie's illness was just another reason to hate it. Lord, was it stupid for her to get embroiled with Preston in an October.

Another look at the clock. Clock-watching wouldn't make him arrive earlier.

Once in the OR, she'd be standing still for hours. She should sit. Or tidy. Yes, tidy some more. There was always something to tidy up. Life got even messier if you let your environment get out of order because uncontrollable forces collided with you.

Of course, all the uncontrollable forces colliding with her meant she didn't have much to tidy *now.* She grabbed her scrub cap and stood waiting as the second hand passed the twelve.

Time to go down. He'd probably changed his mind. Good. She'd tried, given it a day. If he decided against the position now, she wouldn't chase him. She was making up for screwing him over five years ago, not trying to make him like her again. She still didn't need that.

Shaking the right key out of the ring, she exited her office and locked up behind her.

Preston met her at the door.

"You're almost late," Dasha muttered, then remembered she was supposed to be the good one this morning.

"It's called being on time," he drawled.

"I just thought you were an early arriver usually." She clicked the lock and stuffed her keys into her pocket.

His eyes called her on that lie. "Only when you made me be."

"Okay, I thought you'd changed your mind," Dasha said, sighing.

"Were you relieved?" He had his scrub cap in hand. He also had a slight swelling on his left eyelid. "That sounded like disappointment."

"Honestly? A little." Some time last night, while reflecting on her day, Dasha had decided she needed to be honest. Detached and honest. Preston was used to Old Dasha, he didn't appreciate New-and-Improved Dasha much. "What's wrong with your eye?" Someone had hit him, she knew it. She just hoped it wasn't Nettle.

"Nothing you need to worry about."

"Preston, if we're going to do this—"

"Stop. Let me make myself clear." He turned to face her, stopping everything else until he'd spoken. "There is no *we.* We're not doing anything together. We're not friends. We're not rivals. We're not ex-lovers in for a sappy reunion. This is not us building a happy highway into the future together."

She held his gaze, waiting for the rest.

"At the end of the probationary period we'll be people who occasionally stumble across one another at work. If your motives don't jibe with this scenario, tough."

"I have no other motives."

"Fine, you have no other motives."

"You have no reason to believe me, I get it. But

for your own benefit, stow the sarcasm. Stow the aggression," Dasha said. "Make friends, not enemies. No matter what you think of me, if the staff catch you throwing barbs at me, you won't win any points. And just so you know, I'm not the girl I was five years ago. I've grown up. Take my advice. I honestly want you to succeed." She stepped around him and made tracks for the nearest stairwell—moving target, harder to hit.

But that only mattered if he didn't take her advice to heart and didn't throw barbs at her in a public setting where others could hear him. They really wouldn't care for it.

They walked in silence, but no matter how soft his shoes kept his footfalls, she was still unpleasantly aware of the man following. When they reached the room, she held the door for him, as if kind gestures would make him believe she was legit.

He reached the sinks, tied his cap on and turned on the water to start the long process of scrubbing his hands.

She scrubbed in silence, sneaking looks at him in the glass that separated the scrub area from the operating room. Lead by example. Help him build the new paradigm he needed.

"I need to know what happened at Davidson West. I need to know why you fainted." She tried to keep her voice level, emotionless. Or at least nonjudgmental.

"It's complicated." He glanced at her reflection in the glass.

"So is every surgery ever. I can keep up." And please don't say it was booze, drugs, or something else bad.

"And personal," Preston said, his words careful and measured. Careful enough to raise red flags. Swollen eye. Personal fainting issues. It couldn't be drugs.

"Sleep deprivation from something?" She hoped, and scoured her brain for any illnesses presenting with those symptoms, but they just didn't go together. Syncope and swelling… Heart disease?

"Yes." He met her eyes in the reflection, scowled and turned to look at her directly. "Stop it."

"No. What caused it?" She stomped the faucet pedal and with her hands aloft faced him.

"Something. Personal," he reiterated, and then added, "Stop diagnosing me. I know that face."

"Is it your heart?" she asked, and when he started walking tried a different tack. "Are you sleeping better?"

"Like a baby." He flashed a toothy smile at her.

He wanted to drive her nuts. So secretive. "It'd really help me to know what's going on with you."

Apparently Preston had decided he was done talking about it. And now was a really bad time to hit him. Her hands were clean. Her patient was waiting. She followed him out. After getting gowned and gloved, she approached the table and smiled at the large woman lying on her back, staring up at unlit lights.

Time to take her own advice and stow it. She had a patient to put at ease. "Morning, Angie. How're you feeling? Excited?"

Bariatric surgery often made the overweight excited. If the woman hadn't needed surgical help with her weight, they might never have discovered the problem with her twisted and backward intestines until the day it became a life-threatening emergency.

"And nervous," Angie admitted, though her words were a tad slow from the pre-op medication.

"Everything's going to go great," Dasha said, smiling down at her and then nodding to Preston, who'd joined her on the other side of the table, all smiles and charm. "This is a colleague, Dr. Preston Monroe, and he's going to assist in your surgery today."

"Are you a good doctor?" She may be nervous and drugged, but even in that state the woman reacted to Preston's crazy blue eyes with a groggy smile.

Dasha would have laughed if she wasn't irritated with him.

"Number one in my class, Angie." He winked at her.

"How do you know Dr. Hardin?" Angie mumbled.

"We were in school together."

And residency. Hopefully Angie was too out of it to realize that Preston had just taken a roundabout way of saying she wasn't as good a surgeon as he was.

"Dr. Hardin said it's a difficult surgery," Angie garbled.

"She likes to say stuff like that. Makes it seem more impressive later." Preston smiled down at the woman and nodded toward the anesthesiologist at her head. "Time to take a nap."

A little goofy chuckle slipped out of *her* patient, but the anesthesiologist was there with the gas, saving her from a showdown with Preston that Angie would hear.

"I like to be honest with my patients," Dasha muttered. "One hundred percent."

"You were honest."

"And I don't need you cutting me down to them either. They should feel confident in—"

"I wasn't cutting you down," Preston cut in. "It was banter, and it put her at ease. She was confident."

"You charmed her. And you lied," Dasha said, then leaned over and whispered, "which you should do with the staff, not just the patients. Charm them. You know how."

"Relax. If you're worried about the staff liking me, maybe you could act like you do. Set an example," he whispered back.

"Fine," Dasha whispered through gritted teeth, and stepped around to her preferred side for this procedure.

"Malrotation and gastric bypass?"

"Malrotation and sleeve gastrectomy," she corrected in her most cheerful voice, and tried really hard not to consider the irony of the condition for their first scheduled surgery.

Malrotation. Badly twisted-up insides.

Sounded about right.

* * *

Preston pulled his cap off as he exited the OR and made a beeline for the nearest bathroom—his usual routine. Part necessity, part just needing to be alone for a few minutes.

He'd lied to Angie. It was a hard procedure. Long. And he needed to stop fighting with Dasha. It didn't gain him anything. She was right, everyone liked her. No good could come from the antagonism he felt around her. He wanted St. Vincent's. As much as he'd like to pretend otherwise, his surgical skill alone wouldn't get this job for him. And time had repeatedly proved that his skill couldn't keep jobs when his mouth interfered.

On the plus side, at least at the end of day two, he felt firmly reassured that Dasha had the skills to avoid sullying his reputation, or using him to boost her own.

It also felt good to know he'd helped someone. The woman's life would improve. They'd mitigated the danger of an emergency situation in the future.

And his eyes hadn't so much as twitched the whole time. Maybe the injection was going to do the trick. Even if it caused that eye swelling Dasha had grilled him about.

On the way back out, he spotted Dasha and a

male surgeon standing in front of the OR door, speaking in low, heated tones. He leaned and listened, not wanting to interrupt yet. Eavesdropping might not be cool, but this was a public area. If they'd wanted privacy, they should have sought it. It wasn't his fault if they didn't notice him listening.

"You don't have to deal with him," Dasha said, her brows pinched in that way they always had before she got into it with someone.

"I will eventually," the man said. He looked familiar. Maybe. Preston tended to forget any but important faces, and even then sometimes…

"Leave Preston to me. I can manage him." She shifted her weight to her back foot, planting herself. If she hadn't just said she'd manage him, he might be amused at her fighter's stance over a conversation. Someone she actually looked like she might fight with? That didn't fit with her Be Nice, Make Friends motto.

It was the first time he'd seen that look since arriving. The man must be annoying her. If he hadn't been talking about him, Preston might have decided to like the man.

"You only think you can manage him," the man said. "What about everyone else?"

"He's going to do fine. Better than fine. You'll see. You'll be glad he's here," she said.

Dasha was defending him. It took a second for that realization to really penetrate.

"Doubt it," the man said.

"This will all work out." Dasha sounded as put out with this man as she regularly did with him. "Just drop it, Jason."

"His father can't even manage him."

Jason? And knew Davis P.? Oh, hell. Time to interrupt.

"My father stopped managing me when my voice dropped." Preston leaned off the wall and approached. "Preston Monroe." He stuck out one hand, a gesture that was hard for a man to ignore. "You must be Frist."

"I am." Jason Frist, neurosurgeon and golden boy, as far as Preston's father was concerned. The son he'd always wanted. The ideal held up to him when his father lamented his choice of specialty. That Jason. Friends with Dasha too. Or maybe more than that with Dasha. It took a certain kind of closeness to lecture someone.

Frist took Preston's offered hand and gave it a shake. "No offense, man."

Words surged into his throat, but he remembered

his pep talk of minutes ago and stopped the verbal eruption with a choke. He cleared his throat. "You're worried about the department. I get it. You don't need to worry."

"Good to know. I have to be off. Appointments this afternoon. Hardin. Monroe." Frist exited fast, which was something at least. He didn't harp on the subject, and he didn't call Preston on the lip service.

Preston felt Dasha's gaze before he actually saw it, prompting him to turn back to her. "You know, I was coming back here to congratulate you on your performance in surgery and apologize for the situation with Angie, then I heard the conversation and wanted to choke you. You think you can manage me." He folded his arms and leaned one shoulder against the doorjamb.

"You can—"

"And then I saw you defending me," he cut in before she really got going. "Now I don't really know what to think. You looked like you were about to sock Frist in the nose. Did you know I was there?"

"I didn't. But would it make you feel better if I said yes?" She lifted her chin and stared him in the eye. "I'm setting an example." Just when he thought she was gearing up to fight, she smiled at him. A real smile—alight with mischief and challenge. And if he hadn't known what to think before…

She was still in there, beneath all the polish and tact… Before he could think of anything to say, she headed off down the labyrinthine corridors to the stairs she'd taken down from her office. Still a creature of habit. Still someone who could make his belly flip over.

Preston followed. He was on probation with her, this wasn't about him wanting her to smile at him again, because that would be stupid. A couple of quick steps helped him catch up and he looked down at her. "Have you been getting that much?"

"Getting…" Dasha took a few seconds, but soon shook her head. "Not really. If they feel that way, they haven't said anything. I don't expect them to unless you pull a Preston." She grinned again. "Jason's just freer with his words with me."

"You together?" Why did he ask that? It didn't matter who she was with.

Dasha gave him a weird look, but they were only a few steps from the office and she waited until they were inside before she answered, "Why would you ask that? Jason is my friend. We started here around the same time."

"Yes, but your friendship with him links you to my father. Did he put you up to this?"

"I don't know your father, Preston." The weird look turned into a guilty one.

Preston squinted, risking a cascade from those hyperactive eye muscles. "Did he put you up to this? Save his idiot son's career? Because I don't want this position if it's through him."

She paced to the desk and leaned against the front of it, folding her arms over her chest. Hiding something? Or just trying to distract him with—?

"I get that you don't like your dad, but not everyone is his puppet."

Trying to distract him. Definitely trying to distract him. "Direct answer, Dasha. Now." He closed the distance to stand over her, close enough to shake some sense into her if she didn't stop…whatever it was she was doing with her cleavage…

"Your father did not put me up to anything. I do not know him. Jason does not deliver orders or requests on your behalf from Davis Monroe." Dasha stared him in the eye the whole time she spoke, and then for a few seconds after for good measure, daring him not to believe her.

Well, he didn't want to believe her.

Which was really too bad, considering he did believe her.

Still not ready to stop antagonizing her, he continued to hold her eye. "You sure you're not trying to impress Frist and win his tender affections?" It wasn't flirting. It was teasing. Joking around…

Watching her try to decide if he was playing with her or picking a fight tickled him. In the spirit of cooperation, he decided to make it easy on her. "It's okay to want to marry a neurosurgeon and have two point five abnormally brilliant little spawn with him."

"I don't want to marry him," Dasha said slowly, and then shook her head, the smile that came with it more rueful than sparkling. "You haven't changed at all, have you? Just so you know, when you're feeling touchy about something, you have a tendency to joke about it. It's a bad poker face, Preston." She whirled out from between him and the desk, grabbed her bag and headed for the door, bag slung over her shoulder. "We're done for the day."

"Do I? It's because I'm so damned sensitive to the needs of others, everyone can see my concern, no matter what I say."

Did she not get that he was playing with her?

He paused, smile still in place but he had to think about it…make sure that it stayed put so she could pick up on the teasing. She always used to be able to recognize a joke. She'd had a great sense of humor. Aside from the sex and the way she had motivated him, their playfulness had been something he'd never been able to replicate with anyone else. It mattered. Well, it had. Not now…except that it bothered him she'd changed so much, or bothered him that she was pretending to be so different. He wasn't sure which was more accurate, only that he was bothered and she seemed different.

If he could ignore the manner of their parting—and that was something he had to do to even envision this arrangement working—then he had to think about the good things. The idea that he may not have really known her at all rankled more than it should have. More than the betrayal maybe.

He grabbed the strap of the bag as she waltzed by, expecting him to follow, and stopped her in her tracks. "Did you fail to recognize that I'm trying to ease things here with us? Are you really so different now than you used to be? You changed your hair, you changed your wardrobe and you've changed from being direct to beating around the bush to avoid confrontation…but have you lost your sense of humor too? Or was all that an act back then?"

"You're joking now too, right?" She jerked on her bag but he didn't let it go, and from the timbre of her voice he could see she wasn't intent on being tactful. "I always changed my hair—every month, if you recall. I'm wearing work clothes—you can't wear tank tops and flip-flops in your professional life. And being tactful is the way you build relationships with people until you know them well enough to be blunt. That's all part of being an adult."

"And the sense of humor?" Preston held fast to the strap, the only way he knew to keep her in place without actually touching her skin.

She kept enough tension on the bag that the strap was taut, as rigid as her posture. He'd expected her to take a fighter's stance, but again he was wrong. She leaned slightly away from him, partially from the tension she kept on the bag, but it was more than that. Flight. If he let go now, she'd be out the door, leaving him to lock up.

"There's not a lot going on in my life right now that I find funny. And you'll just have to excuse me if having you tease me about dating is one of those things I don't find funny."

"Relax, Dasha." He started to relax his arm, but she kept up the tension on the strap. "Stop pulling."

"You stop pulling." She pulled harder, forcing him to keep his hold.

"You're going to fall over the second I let go. We'll both let go at the same time. On the count of three, okay?" Sadly, this wasn't the most ridiculous confrontation he'd ever gotten into at work. It was just the first time he had gotten into a fight at work where he didn't know he was right from the outset.

The countdown shamed Dasha into compliance. She let go of the bag. Preston didn't fall, but he did bash himself in the cheek when his arm rebounded.

"Right, I'm off," Preston muttered, and dropped the bag on a nearby chair, prowling for the door.

"Wait…" She had to tell him something. What had she…? Oh, right. "Um, Dr. Monroe, we're on call this weekend. I'll call you if we get pulled in for any emergencies."

He nodded and left, leaving her to try and puzzle out what had happened. What had set her off?

Well, there was the questioning of who she was

as a person, as if who she had been had been so much better. How could he even insinuate that after the way things had ended? And he didn't even know New-and-Improved Dasha, so he was just reacting to her being different than he expected.

But that wasn't really what had got her. He'd get to know her now, everyone changed as they matured, and he'd get used to the new her. It had been the joking about Jason that had got to her. She didn't need to explain herself or her current relationship status—or that the only man in her life was her convertible, which she'd named Belvedere for some unfathomable reason…

If she had been interested in Jason—which she wasn't—that wouldn't be cheating on Preston. But in the moments after he'd teased her about it that's what she'd felt like. That's what it still felt like. And if that told her anything, it was that though her methods in the past had not been right, she really did have to go to extremes to stay away from him. She hadn't set eyes on him for five years, and she still felt like she belonged to him. So stupid…

Twenty minutes later Dasha climbed into her car.

To hell with running today. She should visit Marjorie and Bill. No call duty tonight, but tomorrow she'd be on and planning anything on a call weekend never worked out.

Plus, she wanted to go. Sort of.

Every time she visited, Marjorie was a little further gone. Asleep a little longer. Voice a little weaker. And it became a little harder for Dasha to hold on to the scrap of hope that she'd turn this disease around.

She'd heard about miraculous cures, inexplicable spontaneous remissions, but she'd never witnessed one. Now she stood at the edge of losing her second mother. The trauma surgeon who'd tried so hard to save Dasha's mother, and who had cried with her when she hadn't been able to. And who'd remembered Dasha and taken her under her wing after she'd selfishly thrown Preston to the wolves to make sure she could get to St. Vincent's.

And she was once again being selfish by thinking about how Marjorie's imminent death affected *her.* Me, me, me.

Flowers. She should get flowers.

Or donuts.

Or both.

At least it was something to do, kept her from feeling helpless.

Half an hour later Dasha slipped into the bedroom and joined Bill, sitting by the bed, watching Marjorie sleep. She made her customary check of the equipment and room, making sure everything was as it should be, and then plopped onto the arm of his chair.

"He's giving you a run for your money, eh?" Bill murmured.

"That obvious?" Dasha whispered back, not wanting to disturb Marjorie.

"The sigh gave it away."

"Didn't realize I'd sighed." She slouched, dropping her bag onto the floor. "He just sort of dredges up everything again. I'd like to stick with the here and now, but it's looking less and less likely that I'll be able to do that."

Bill winced. He knew everything Marjorie knew, and Marjorie knew it all. All the way down to her getting out before she'd ended up turning into her mother—devoted to a man she could never have.

"Don't worry. I didn't hit him. He kind of hit himself after we had some kind of showdown over my bag, though." Yeah, that would help him not worry. Perfect. "I don't know exactly how that happened, but he was joking around with me. I don't know why he was. Maybe because of Jason."

"Jason giving you trouble?" Bill's frown didn't express a lack of worry. Still not helping.

"Not exactly. He's just worried about Preston causing trouble. And Preston kind of caught Jason talking about him."

"Heaven help us. Did you get it sorted out?"

"I think so." Dasha shrugged. She really wasn't going to mention Nettle.

"I'm sorry I can't be there to help with the situation," Bill said.

"Don't. It's nothing you should apologize for. You're right where you need to be." She squeezed his hand. "It's nothing you should have to get involved with anyway. My doing. All mine." She thought for a moment and added, "And his father's not helping. I don't know exactly what happened between the two of them, but he said some things that makes me think they have a kind of feud."

"The senior Monroe meddles," Bill murmured. "We were surprised when you got the fellowship. Davis had arranged for it to go to Preston. All he had to do was show up that day."

Dasha's jaw dropped and her stomach curdled. "Why...you never said anything."

"Would you have felt better?" Bill asked, leaning forward in the chair so he could hold her gaze better as they talked.

"No." It didn't really change anything. If anything, it would have made her less certain of Preston's opportunities. "Probably worse."

Bill nodded, not elaborating. They'd been protecting her. She still never expected that from anyone, even after the past years of being included in Marjorie and Bill's lives, even with those she loved, she never expected protection.

"I think I need to stretch my legs." He stood, and then gestured her to slide into the seat…and off the arm of his favorite chair. "Will you stay?"

She nodded, his revelation spinning in her head.

"Later I'm making my famous takeout," he said as he wandered toward the door, talking to himself now more than her. "Mexican, I think. Feels like a taco kind of day."

It felt more like a burrito day to her. Wrapped up, confined, lots of messy stuff hidden beneath a pretty, soft, white, flavorless case.

Why tell her now? To protect her? To give her extra fortitude she'd need to handle whatever Preston threw at her? Or maybe because he'd just known she was ready to hear it. How nice would it be for a relationship man to get her that way?

She'd have to let them know her better for that to happen.

Did Preston even know about the fellowship? Might explain why he thought that Davis was manipulating her into giving him the job.

Well, if he didn't know, she couldn't tell him. It didn't matter, not really. She'd done what she'd done, and saying that he would have gotten it because of his father just sounded like a cop-out. She hadn't known, she'd just assumed he'd get it because he was better than her. And then she'd consoled herself with the knowledge that he'd have tons of other opportunities, and she needed St. Vincent's.

No good could come from telling him. Best case scenario, it would just give him something else to resent his father over.

"You're frowning."

Dasha looked up when she heard Marjorie's voice, and then rose to go sit on the edge of the bed. "I'm practicing looking serious and formidable."

"What are you really thinking?" Marjorie smiled.

"Thinking other less productive things." Dasha smoothed the blankets down, tucking and tidying. "I got the invitation for the winter ball today.

I'm thinking of getting something classy to wear in honor of the fancy-pants hotel where it's held. You know, slit up to here and down to there, and covered in sequins. I'm thinking orange with lime-green accessories."

"You should be thinking escorts and not trying to scandalize me with your fluorescent monstrosities," Marjorie murmured.

She was smiling, though. Dasha would probably wear that hideously described dress if it would make Marjorie smile. "Hair teased out high enough for squirrels to nest in."

"And a top hat."

Dasha's turn to laugh. "Hair teased into the shape of a top hat."

"Enough foolishness now. How are you doing with Preston?"

"Oh, well…I really have no idea. Mercurial as ever. Evasive then charming. Antagonistic and then playful. I really have no idea. He's still there and no one has filed any official complaints. At least, not that I know of."

"That's not what I'm talking about, Dasha."

"He joked with me earlier. And I yelled at him a little bit." That story lost something in translation.

"Why?"

"It was… I don't know. I'm not entirely sure what happened." Dasha waved a hand in the air, trying to get past the subject she suffered a lack of words on. "Don't worry. I'm not giving up yet, and he might not go nuclear on me."

"You need to figure it out, honey. Even if you don't want to dwell on it," Marjorie advised, and then in her soothing way followed on by addressing the needs of the other soul in her care. "Bill's said no to outside nursing, but I want you to talk him into getting someone to come in here at night. He's not sleeping like he should."

"Okay. I'll make sure it's someone good." Dasha leaned in and kissed Marjorie on the cheek, her throat suddenly thick enough to make her voice raspy. "Just until you're well enough to look after him yourself."

She had to hold on to the idea of a miraculous recovery.

CHAPTER THREE

FLOOR-TO-CEILING windows ran the entire length of Preston's loft, which had been converted from a nineteenth-century third-floor warehouse in the heart of historic downtown Nashville—where much of Nashville's night-life now was located.

The glow from neon signs and streetlights illuminated his apartment in soothing blues and greens, and unless he had to read something or stab himself in the eye with a needle Preston left the lights off. Even while working out on his climbing machine.

It also made him feel a little better, a salve to his ego, that the low lighting at least downplayed the pink flowers on the stupid gel mask he'd resorted to wearing. The woman at the pharmacy had claimed it soothed tired eyes, but so far he didn't feel soothed. And neither did his eyes. He might as well have bought pantyhose, feminine hygiene products and something with wings—whatever those were.

So much for the injections fixing the problem. One day. One freaking day without any symptoms, was that too much to ask? Today it had kicked up again, not even at the hospital this time. That was something. He'd noticed the feeling as soon as he'd opened his eyes, so it had started when he'd been asleep. Either that, or he so strongly remembered the sensation he'd worked himself up a phantom leg type of situation.

Whatever the reason, it wasn't good. He couldn't do another round of injections already and his attempts to manage it with medication worked about as well. Time for more aggressive tactics—before he lost everything. That possibility seemed more real with the eye situation than it ever had because of his mouth. Felt more personal too. Like a real failing rather than being unable to suffer idiots.

He climbed faster. Running built great endurance, but did nothing for the upper body. And did equally little to help him work out the aggression he'd been feeling of late.

Saturday, on call and nearing evening, it looked like he might have a reprieve. Strange that there'd been no calls. Maybe Dasha just hadn't called him in.

Maybe it was a hint that he should cut and run.

His constant failing on personal vows to maintain professional distance with her said he wasn't as over her as he wanted to believe. He swung from baiting her to flirting with her to growling at her. Out of his damned mind.

And he probably had to take some responsibility in everyone trying to manage him all the time. Maybe telling people when they were being idiots wasn't the best career move ever. And he had to make this work. He loved Nashville. He didn't want to move.

And he didn't want to play games with Dasha.

His cell rang and Preston climbed down from the machine to answer it, his body thrumming with the exertion.

Dasha.

Trauma surgical call. Either she wasn't avoiding him or it had been a slow weekend.

A short, clipped conversation, and he jogged to the bathroom to towel off. No time for a full shower, but he could get rid of some stench, put on fresh scrubs and be out the door in less than five minutes. That would put him arriving ahead of her anyway, as the tags on her car told him she lived outside the county. Further away than he did. But he'd inherited the District apartment from his grandfather. She'd probably had to buy her own place, and that wasn't cheap in the metro area. Not anymore. The ever-growing city ate up real estate.

Fifteen minutes later he stood in Emergency, getting briefed.

Patient: Jason Frist.

He felt fleeting pride for having refrained from saying anything he'd wanted to say to his father's protégé yesterday. And then he felt something else: the dark foreboding that accompanied the knowledge his father would be coming. The old man would be at the hospital as soon as he heard of Frist's accident. No rolling that to voice mail.

And with their friendship, should Dasha even be the one operating?

He dialed her cell.

"I'm just walking in the door," she said, sounding breathy and more like she was running in the door than walking.

"I've been briefed. It's Frist. You need to get someone else. Or let me do it," Preston said, adding, "I'm scrubbing in OR Three." He rang off, crammed his surgical cap on his head and started the scrub. Inside the OR people hovered, monitoring the hospital's neurosurgeon.

"I'm here." Dasha ran in, tying her cap on. "What's going on?"

"He fell. I don't know the details. Someone said he was going to pick apples today. Guessing he hit some limbs on the way down. Abdominal trauma. Internal bleeding. Probable splenic rupture. He's losing blood. He's got some broken bones too." But the life-threatening issues came first, orthopedics followed when the patient had stabilized.

Preston was ahead of her in the scrubbing procedure and he went on into the OR, not waiting. As soon as he was outfitted, he pulled back the drape to examine the man.

This was important, with everyone tense, he had to be gentle with them, get the performance he needed from them, make sure Dasha's head stayed in the game and pull the neurosurgeon through. The second doctor in an accident that week, and staff were more than on edge because of it. He needed to do all he'd failed to do yesterday.

He prodded the abdomen lightly, feeling distinct swelling in one area, hardening in another. "Dasha, I can handle this." He called toward the open door to the scrub room. "You're emotionally attached."

"I'm fine, Preston. He'd want me in there."

"And if he dies?" Preston had to speak louder to

make sure she heard him, and those really weren't the words to shout around Frist's friends. Everyone winced. But he needed to be sure.

"He won't." Was that faith? Or just denial?

"Dr. Hardin." He tried again.

"Then a friend dies." She scrubbed with gusto. "We'll see him through this. You start. I'm right behind you."

Through the glass, he could see the emotion on her face. Worried. A little grim. But not pale and teetering on the edge of a nervous breakdown. Maybe she really had no romantic interest in the man. Or maybe the same emotional mechanism that had allowed her to stab him in the back allowed her the distance she needed now.

"All right." He frowned, but went out to get gloved and gowned. "Is he out?" He looked at the anesthesiologist, who nodded. His right eye twitched, the third time since he'd arrived.

"He was in a lot of pain. And his consciousness was touch and go anyway," the man said.

Preston looked at the nurse, who handed him his preferred scalpel, already learning to anticipate his needs. Now he just needed his eyes to perform at the same level.

Dasha bellied up to the left side of the bed as Preston began the initial incision.

And had another twitch.

Dammit.

Could she handle cutting into a friend without backup? Without him? The determined look in her eyes as she swabbed the bleeding said she could. Steady hand and a focused gaze…that noticed his hand stopping.

"Dr. Monroe?"

It was just a single twitch. Not the end of the world. Just a twitch.

Just a twitch that he couldn't risk his patient for.

He handed the scalpel to her and reached for clamps and sponges to start controlling the blood. She worked cleanly and fast, and with two good eyes and hands. He tried to turn off the doubts blackening the edge of his mood. This was just like Davidson West. Everyone would know. His career would be over. This was the one thing he did—the one thing he was—that was of value to the world.

His twitching increased enough to compromise his vision, and at that second he backed away from the table. The nurse beside him stepped in with a curious glance and suction, putting her questions aside to keep the team choreography smooth.

Hoping his eye would settle, he did other stuff. Managed information. How many units of Jason's blood type did they have on hand? How many had he gone through? What were his vitals like?

"Preston." Dasha said his name in a way that suggested she'd said it more than once.

"Yes." His left eye was blinking in multisecond bursts every ten to fifteen seconds.

"Are you all right? If you're not with me, I need you to get me another set of hands in here."

"Of course. Feeling ill suddenly. I'll make the call." Hello, it's my third day and I'm already failing my duties…

"Thank you." She glanced up at him, frowned and added, "We'll be okay."

Dasha kept her eyes on him a moment longer than she really should have, but only long enough to let him know she was on to him.

Grabbing the phone on the wall, he made a quick call and arranged for better hands—better heads—to assist her. God, it was going to cripple him. Ruin him forever. They liked to say a surgeon was only as good as his hands, but the eyes were just as important.

He made his way around the table. "Keys," he whispered in Dasha's ear, before sliding his hand around her firm, rounded hip and into her pocket. His body came alive from the heat he felt through the thin material, even with his attention focused on getting out. She stiffened, and, God help him, so did he. That hurried him up, making him a touch clumsy.

This was just a need for comfort. Any attractive woman would elicit the same reaction from him in his current state of mind. Even as he reassured himself, he knew it was a lie. She still had some kind of power over him.

Keys in hand, he headed out through the scrub room. His mask and gown hit the bin and he was about to step out when he noticed Dasha's gym bag. And, more importantly, the sunglasses tucked in the end pocket. At least something was going his way.

He snagged the bag, snatched the sunglasses out and put them on. A little small, but they'd do.

By the time he was in the hall, the right eye had joined the left, and both blinked rapidly.

He muddled his way down the hall and into a stairwell, then moved to stand beneath the metal stairs in the only place people weren't likely to see his eyes—even if they noticed him lurking beneath the stairs in a creepy fashion. More importantly, the harsh lighting didn't reach that space either, providing meager relief for the headache forming.

If his eyes blinked together, that would be one thing. But each had its own rhythm, a feat he couldn't manage consciously even if he tried.

His father would be on his way to the hospital. He'd hear that his son had bowed out of the surgery on the World's Most Amazing Mentee, and then it really wouldn't matter what Dasha had to say about this episode—Davis P. Monroe would have some special extra-ashamed words for him. Like he didn't have the sense to recognize this nightmare poking him in the eye.

He made his way out from under the stairs and, grabbing the rail, walked slowly up. Fifth floor. He needed to reach the fifth floor, and find his way down the several corridors that would take him to Dasha's office. There he could shut off the lights, lock the door, close the blinds and wait for it to pass.

The only way the situation could be remotely tolerable was in the dark, when he wasn't bombarded with flickering snapshots of the world around him.

And he needed to do it without anyone finding him out.

He'd have to thank Dasha later for being an anal, overorganized, overprepared loon.

A good two hours later Dasha stepped out of the OR and went to find Jason's family. Instead, she found Dr. Davis P. Monroe, alone in the surgical waiting room, looking every bit as fierce and disapproving as she'd last seen him—the day she'd sold her soul for the fellowship and eventual position at St. Vincent's.

After she'd got Preston stinking drunk, loved him as only a woman saying goodbye could and left him handcuffed to his bed so he'd miss their joint interview and she'd get the position. The position she now knew that this man had already arranged for Preston—who thought so little of his son he didn't know what an amazing surgeon he'd raised and trust him to stand on his own achievements.

How should she feel about that? Did she even have the right to feel the outrage she felt on Preston's behalf? No, this scheme had begun as penance—but getting Preston into St. Vincent's had turned into something else in the last few days. Something she wasn't ready to slap a label on.

Reaching Preston's father, she said, "Dr. Monroe, I know you're here for Jason, but is his family here as well? Or on the way?" She didn't know them, but she knew the man they had raised and had seen the yearly goofy Christmas-sweater portrait cards Jason sent out. They were like the Waltons. They'd be there if they knew.

"Out of town," Dr. Monroe said, standing. Despite the open, modern layout of the waiting area, he still managed to dominate the space. Did he know what she'd done? She knew what he'd done—and really didn't care what he thought of her suddenly. They'd both wronged Preston. "I'm the only one here for Jason. How is he doing? I was told my son was part of the procedure."

"I'm sorry, sir, but you know I can't talk about his case with you." HIPPA laws, and all that. "I'll call his family and ask them to give you a call."

"No. You'll tell me. I'm an emergency contact." He made a cutting motion with his hand, effectively silencing her. She couldn't tell whether he was aggravated that Jason was hurt or worried, but she could see he didn't like being told no.

"He's doing well," she said slowly, standing up a little straighter, readying herself for battle if she had to fight. "Please excuse me for one moment." She fished her phone from her pocket, turned away and double-checked Jason's information for the emergency contact names. There he was. Okay. Time to stop thinking like Preston with regard to the man. Think about Jason. This is about Jason. "We removed the spleen, stopped all the bleeding. After he's stabilized, Orthopedics will have to go in and repair his arm and left leg. He was picking apples, I'm told. Left side of his body is beat all to hell."

"His hand?" Monroe asked, taking it all in with the same determined frown she'd seen on Preston.

"I'm not sure, honestly. I was more concerned with getting the spleen out and making sure nothing else was bleeding. I know they put in a central line rather than an IV in his extremities, both left limbs are broken, but they could be clean breaks. Whatever fractures he has, none are compound." Though knowing how bashing damage could mangle a body, those bones could be shattered. He knew too, but he could show a little more concern for his friend's life and less for his dexterity. "I'm sorry I can't give you more information about the orthopedic prognosis. I can find out, or at least find the right people to come and talk to you."

"Do that," Monroe said, and then asked again, "Where's Preston? Wasn't he in the surgery?"

"He was, but he had to leave." Don't lie. And don't give him anything to be suspicious about. Don't give him anything to growl at Preston about. "I don't think he knew you were waiting." Not that he would have come if he had known, she felt sure of that.

"Fine. I'll phone him. Go find the orthopedic surgeon, someone who knows what he's talking about."

Dismissed. Dasha took that exit and raced for the office. She dug her phone from her back pocket and called Preston.

He answered her call.

"Where are you? Do you have my bag? I need my bag and my keys."

"I have them. They're safe. Go and get something to eat and then find me." Preston hung up, the second Monroe in a row to give her orders.

She rang him back. "We got disconnected."

"We were done talking," Preston said.

"No, we weren't done—"

He hung up again.

"Son of a— Jumpin' monkey knuckles!" New-and-Improved Dasha didn't cuss a blue streak when she was upset. New-and-Improved Dasha also couldn't come up with suitable substitute words when upset either. She should probably sit down and brainstorm some good alternative swear words for times like this. Planning ahead kept things tidy.

She rang him again. “I swear if you hang up on me, I’m going to kill you, Preston Monroe.”

“Kill me later. Like in half an hour.”

“No. Now. And then I’m going to knock your father on the head with something heavy. Where are you?” She pounded up the stairs, because she had to keep moving and there was a chance he was in the office.

“Your office.”

Yes!

“Go get something to eat. Or coffee. Something. Come back in half an hour,” he commanded again. Like she’d forgotten in the last thirty seconds.

“The hell I will. Besides, I can’t go to the cafeteria. My purse is in that bag you swiped.”

“Then just go for a walk.” Preston offered an alternative command. Did he think she was bringing his father with her? She’d just expressed her desire to smash his father’s big swollen head with something!

Reaching the office door, she tried the knob. Of course it was locked.

“Let me in, Preston,” she snarled into the phone.

"In a while." He hung up.

"I'm going to get Security to let me in if you don't open the...*f—freaking* door!" she called through the closed thing and rattled the knob. *Don't drop an F-bomb. Don't drop an F-bomb...*

Getting no response, she picked up her phone again and called Maintenance.

Ten minutes later she opened the door and stepped inside.

All the lights were off.

She let the door swing shut and reached for the lights, then immediately wished she hadn't.

"Dammit, Dasha. Turn off the lights and go away," Preston barked from across the office, sitting in the desk chair currently swiveled away from her.

The plants that had once sat on the windowsill were now variously strewn about. Some on the floor. Some hanging far enough over the edge of the desk that they'd be on the floor if someone sneezed on them. No doubt he'd moved them to close the blinds, all of which were down and the slats rolled tightly shut.

"God, what are you doing in here?"

"Nothing."

"Are you going through my stuff?" Dasha forced

the words through gritted teeth, saving the plants and pretending that was the completely rational question to ask.

"No. I'm sitting. Now turn off the lights." He sounded as frustrated as she felt.

Ignoring his demand, she scurried about, at least grouping the plants all in one safe place. A mess. He was messing up everything.

"Turn off the lights!" His voice rose.

"This is my office. Not yours," Dasha reminded him, then added, "Your father is downstairs."

"You called my father?" He swiveled around as he yelled, giving her a first look at his face.

At his eyes.

"No." The word creaked out, all anger sucked out at that second. "He's Jason's contact in town."

He hadn't been kidding when he'd said he was unwell. She headed back to the door and flipped the lights off. Then for good measure, and to make sure his jerk of a father didn't just stroll in looking for him, she relocked the door.

Across the cavernous darkness she asked, "What's going on with your eyes?"

"Nothing."

"Oh, is this just a party trick, then?" Dasha moved slowly across the dark office.

"It's idiopathic." Her sarcasm worked. "At least I can't find a reason for it." He sighed, the anger draining out of his voice. Weary. He sounded so weary.

For a moment she didn't know what to say. Or if she should say anything. What could she do to help him? Find out details. Diagnose. Cure. Simple steps she knew how to do. With most people. "How long has this been going on?"

"Couple…a few weeks."

A few weeks meant it could still clear up on its own. That was possible. She'd heard of fleeting and inexplicable dystonia before. "The swelling?"

"My first botulin injection."

"You did it yourself?" Dasha asked. He certainly hadn't asked her or his father to do it.

He paused and she knew the answer. She made her way around the table she'd grouped the plants on. The office layout was etched in her memory, she'd paced it enough this week. And even in past years when she'd worked there with Bill, wandering the open spaces without looking, eyes fixed on whatever she happened to be reading. Being überorganized didn't hurt. She made it to the desk and around to where Preston sat in heavy silence.

"Is it painful?" She rested a hip against the edge

of the desk, trying to affect a casual stance before remembering that he couldn't see her casual stance.

"Not exactly."

"The lights?" Getting information from him would probably require prompting the whole way.

"It's easier to suffer in the dark. I notice it less." Her eyes adjusted enough for her to see him lift one shoulder. Shrugs were frequently a sign of distress. "More psychological pain than physiological, except right now my eyes are feeling sensitive to light too. I think. Or maybe I'm just losing my mind."

This condition would freak her out, but he was trying to manage it on his own. Didn't he have anyone at all he could get help from?

She eased onto the desk so she could be close to where he sat, facing him. "Preston, I think I know the answer, but is this what happened at Davidson West?"

"More or less," he muttered, sounding very tired. "They locked closed that day. Some days it's like they just refuse to open. But some days it's this. I thought I was getting a handle on it."

"If it's neurological, your dad might—"

"No. Dash, you can't tell him." His voice was strained. "I don't want him involved."

Dasha wished with all her might that she could see him right then. And that must be what it was like for him when this happened to his eyes.

"I don't want to talk right now. Just let me sit. Go and get something to eat, and let me sit until it passes."

"I'll go if you want me to, but I'd rather stay." Holding to that would be hard, she really didn't want to leave him here. "I know you don't have any reason to trust me, but I don't think you should be alone right now."

"I'll be fine," Preston said, his voice almost gone, just a hair above whispering.

"Will you be worse if I stay?" He never showed weakness. Never. If he got knocked down, he came up swinging. All except that time when she'd messed things up between them forever.

"Can you be quiet?" he asked.

"I can be quiet." She leaned off the desk. A quick trip around and she fetched a chair to carry back to where he sat. With the chair nearby, she sat and laid her head back to stare into the blackness. At night, with her shades down, it really was a dark office. Another layer of protection to keep him from seeing the guilt on her face. It was there.

New-and-Improved Dasha might dress better, have a great career and a warm, homey little cottage, but since she'd begun letting herself feel anything but anger, she'd become crap at keeping feelings off her face.

In the dark, she became acutely aware of how badly she wanted to touch him. He wouldn't appreciate it if she caved in to that urge.

These thoughts weren't helping. Dasha forced her mind to the disease, trying to remember anything she could about blepharospasm. Neurological. Sometimes idiopathic. Sometimes treated with medications, though she couldn't say what they were. Botulin injections could help, but maybe it took a while? She couldn't remember.

Her knees started to bounce.

"Dash? Be still."

"I'm sorry." She was. About so much. About things he might never be able to accept an apology over, but she could apologize for this. Her lower lip quivered, and kept her from saying anything else.

"Are you crying?"

"No." A lie.

"It sounds like you're crying." She could hear

his frown, so why would he not hear the weakness in her voice?

"I'm not." She lied some more and tried to breathe more evenly. This wasn't about her—she had to stop being so selfish about these things. He needed help. He needed someone.

But if the condition wiped out his career at the time he was finally getting to be where he should've always been…

"Stop it," he grumbled, but there was no anger there.

Slowly she reached out and laid her hand over his. Strong hands. Warm. Long fingers. The hands of a musician, and the mouth of a madman.

She tried to breathe through her rapidly swelling nose.

"Stop." He turned his hand over and let her link her fingers with his.

Good. It felt good. She was supposed to be the one giving comfort, not the other way around. "I'm stopping."

"You can't tell anyone," he whispered.

"Preston."

"Please."

He never said please. The enormity of the word filled her throat.

"You owe that to me, Dasha."

Yes, she owed him, but she should help him. Ignoring this problem wouldn't cure it. "I'll try to help you keep it secret, but you have to seek treatment." What else could she do? Betray him a second time by not respecting his wishes in this? Steer him in the right direction and pray he didn't buck her suggestions just because he could?

"I'll think about it."

Talking about his problem seemed gentler than attacking his inability to trust anyone with it. "Did you inject in both eyes before?"

"No, just the left."

The swollen one.

"Let me do the right one later, since they both seem to be on the blink. At least it will be safer than self-injecting." She paused and then added, "Sorry about the bad pun."

"Okay." Not arguing was a good sign. "You said you could be quiet."

"I can be quiet." She whispered the words again, and turned her mind off the Preston situation. Just sit. Feel the strength in his hand. Be his support. Why didn't he want anyone to know? He could have time to recover if he needed it. St. Vincent's would give him that time.

Later. She'd ask those questions later. Right now she was supposed to be being quiet. At least on the outside. Inside her mind was entirely different. She'd never been able to shut that voice down. Guilt came with a megaphone.

The fact that he had bowed out of today's surgery when things had got bad for him told her he was still putting patients first, but what happened if his episodes increased? What if he couldn't perform any surgeries?

She took a deep breath. What-ifs could wreck her ability to comfort. She just had to give him whatever he would take right now. Her touch. Keeping his secret until he was ready to share. Her help, if he would accept it.

"You can't be quiet, can you?" He almost sounded amused.

"I didn't say anything."

"No. But you've sighed three times in the last couple of minutes."

Sigh control had never been part of her Dasha Renovation plans. New-and-Improved Dasha sighed a lot, apparently. "I guess I can't be quiet."

"Then could you go?"

"I can't just leave you like this." Don't bring up the other time, don't bring up the other time…

"Dash."

Change the subject! "It could be worse, you know."

"Do tell."

Maybe she could distract him. "You could be losing your hair too."

This time he didn't laugh. Had she found something he couldn't laugh about?

A couple of seconds after she thought she'd further upset him, he murmured, "You think I couldn't pull off bald?" He was smiling. She could hear it in his voice. His hand had relaxed a touch too. Maybe he really couldn't understand subjects too close to home to laugh about.

"I don't know. I have a razor in my desk, though. We could give it a shot." She squeezed his hand. "As we're waiting, I mean."

"My scrub cap would become totally unnecessary."

"It's false advertising anyway. Or do you drive a Harley-Davidson now?"

"I don't have to own a bike to pull off the Harley cap. I'm that badass."

Now she was smiling. "Yeah, yeah, keep dreaming, Chopper."

Stupid jokes, but it eased him. She could feel the

tension draining from him in the way his fingers relaxed and their joined hands melded together.

It didn't last. There was something else there. A current, like electricity vibrating in the air after a lightning strike. Ominous and full of anticipation. Or the smell of ozone that saturated everything in the first minutes of a summer storm—when the world seems a little bit strange. Brighter. Fresher. Sharper.

He felt it too. His breathing sped up. Say something.

"I'm not very good at comforting people," Dasha said, and loosened her hand, preparing to let his go.

"Depends on your frame of reference," he said. What did that mean?

"Okay…I'm not as good at comforting as Marjorie is. She makes it…effortless. I don't know how to do that without making it about me." Or that's how it seemed to her. "About how someone else's misfortune makes me sad for them."

"Experiencing an emotion doesn't make you selfish," Preston said, not letting go of her hand yet. "That's the difference between empathy and pity. And that's the reason I'm not throwing you out right now."

"Thank you for that. I need to be here…and that

is about me, even if the empathy isn't selfish," she said softly, letting her fingers curl back into his and the pad of her thumb stroke up the side of his finger.

He didn't say anything. He probably didn't have any better idea of what to say than she did. They didn't fit, personalities, backgrounds…but their hands fit.

It was even the same position their hands had always taken, his thumb on the outside. His hands were a great deal bigger than hers so it was natural that they'd take that same position when linked together. Not habit. She could move her thumb to the outside if she wanted…

But she didn't want to.

The last thing she should be doing was caressing his hands. The familiar friction and heat, the long, square fingers caused an ache in her chest so sharp she very nearly lost the battle with tears.

A focus, she needed a goal. Touching and thinking about him, about the past, about the way she still missed him wasn't the way to keep from getting weepy and sentimental. She needed a task.

Swallowing it all down, Dasha stood and pushed between him and the desk, keeping his hand in hers as she repositioned herself.

"What are you doing?"

"Hand massage. It's good for stress." Dasha edged onto the desk and wiggled her fingers free of his.

"I don't need a hand massage."

"Do you want me to be quiet?"

"Yes."

"Then hush and let me do this." Her eyes had adjusted to the dark well enough to make out rough outlines, but it was enough. She didn't want to look at him. Think about someone else. Pretend he was a patient. Her fingers pressed and worked the muscles of his palm, rolling over the ball of his thumb.

His breathing hitched higher.

He let her stroke, squeeze and manipulate his hand for several minutes, and the task kept her mouth from running on autopilot, but when she reached for the other hand, he caught hers and pulled. "Be direct, Dasha. If you really want to comfort me..."

"Preston—"

Before his name had fully left her lips he dragged her into his lap, strong hands transferring from hers to the back of her head. Fingers plowed beneath the band of her ponytail, steering her mouth to his.

Dasha's mind blanked. Frustration and uncertainty, fear and guilt, all those treacherous emotions that had tainted every thought she'd had of him for years, drained away. Her mouth opened to his tongue. In surrendering, the onslaught gentled, but his kiss still battered her senses. The heat of his body seeped into her, and she couldn't tell whether it was his heart or hers hammering against her sternum.

Her senses filled up, she could stay there. Not thinking. Pressed against his solid frame, letting him banish every thought, especially the vulnerability she'd been allowed to witness. With hazy intentions, her hands roved over his chest, fingers dipping into the V-neck of his scrubs to find and luxuriate in the firm male flesh and the crispness of the hair dusting his chest.

She wanted to feel more—discover how five years had changed him.

She wanted his chest against hers, skin to skin.

She wanted to hear those urgent sounds that had always told her how much he wanted her too. At least in that way he'd always wanted to know everything about her. Share every pleasure, every breath.

She wanted…

The door to rattle.

"Dr. Hardin?" a male voice called through the locked door.

Someone outside the office?

Preston jerked to a standing position so fast she'd have been dumped on the floor if she hadn't had one arm anchored around his shoulders.

"God, he's tenacious," Preston whispered against her ear.

Busted.

How surreal. Parents were supposed to interrupt sexy make-out sessions before their children were old enough to vote. And never ever after that.

"I forgot about him," Dasha admitted, keeping her own voice in the same conspiratorial whisper. She looked over her shoulder into the dark office. She could see better now that her amygdala had sharpened her vision as an overreaction to nonexistent danger.

"What do we do?" she hissed in his ear, peeling her arms from his shoulders. Whatever they'd been about to do felt entirely too scandalous while hiding in a dark office for no good reason.

"Be quiet and hope he leaves," Preston whispered back. It was his favorite maneuver for dealing with Davis P. Usually it applied to his phone, though. Don't answer. His father didn't usually chase after him on foot. But, then, he wasn't chasing Preston. He was after Dasha. "What does he want?"

"I was supposed to find Jason's orthopedic surgeon to come talk prognosis for the hand."

Whoops. Well, to be fair, she had probably been distracted by his issues. For whatever reason.

When he saw the look on her face, Preston realized the strobelike vision had passed. He could clearly see every inch of surprise and arousal battling for control of her lovely features. Her ponytail hung askew with a bunch of hair having pulled loose.

"Crap crap crap."

Crap? Was that the way she swore now? She used to have much less control of her mouth. Then she'd had less control of everything. Except him. She'd had really good control of him.

What the hell had he been thinking, making out with Dasha? That had never worked out well for him.

"I'm sure that's what he wants. If you're going out, better take your hair down. You look…really sexy." Even in the dark he could see her blush.

"Dammit."

That was more like it.

She tugged the band from her hair and swiped her hand over her mouth a few times, like he'd been wearing lipstick or something.

"I don't have cooties, Dasha." His father knocked again. Did the man hear them whispering?

"You don't have to." She breathed the words. "I probably have kiss mouth."

"Kiss mouth?"

"Pink. Puffy." She shook her head and raised her voice to call at the door, "Just a second!"

Now he knew they were there. "You suck at hiding. Don't invite him in."

"Or tell him you're in here. I got it. I'm not stupid," she whispered back to him, grabbing her bag and her keys. Before she moved out of whisper range she shot at him, "Don't drive until you're better. And lock the door behind you." Then she stepped out.

No goodbye. Just as well considering how tempted he was to kiss her again. The door clicked shut. Wait five minutes and then get the hell out of there. Go home. Drink beer.

God, he could still taste her.

CHAPTER FOUR

MONDAY MORNING DAWNED bright and clear, a diversion from the cold soupy mornings of the preceding week. When Dasha arrived at St. Vincent's, Preston had beaten her there and stood at the head of her special temporary parking place that came with her special temporary office.

Met outside? Not ominous at all. "Morning," she mumbled, locking up and then turning her attention on him. "What's up?"

He patted the backpack slung over one shoulder. "I got the stuff."

Right. Part of his secret-keeping agenda. The man really wasn't cut out to be a secret agent. "Good. Office?"

He shrugged. He may have met her outside but it wasn't because he wanted to see or be near her. As they walked, he maintained a conspicuous distance between them.

Since the episode on Saturday, they hadn't spoken. Dasha had spent her Sunday visiting Marjorie and Bill and praying she didn't get called into the hospital because yet another St. Vincent's doctor had gotten hurt.

She'd been called in for a short surgery early and hadn't had the will to call Preston. There was just too much going on in her mind to let it be polluted with sex. Besides, she'd suppressed that part of herself for years—suppressed or lost interest. Probably some war of self-punishment levied on her by her conscience. And now that he'd returned to her life? The best way to continue torturing herself involved her libido going supernova anytime he was near.

Two major people in her life were unwell, she'd taken on the responsibility of running the department, was busily wrestling demons from her past and also helping Preston with his issue—no room for any other emotions. No room for anything else in her schedule. If she failed any aspect of this, she may as well kiss her job goodbye. The board had told her in no uncertain terms they didn't want him, and after she'd begged and Bill had given a recommendation, they'd agreed on the grounds that should Preston erupt in his usual fashion, she'd be the sacrificial lamb Legal and Public Relations would need to fix the matter.

"You aren't your usual polished self this morning," Preston said, but it didn't sound like a jab for once.

"No." Maybe she shouldn't have skipped the foundation and blush. She had only had mascara and lipstick in her purse when she'd decided to stay over at the Saunders's. She'd have stayed the day too if she could have. "I'm not in a good mood either. So…"

"I see." People passed between them as they navigated the beautiful blue granite hallways branching off the main lobby. They continued apart and in silence until they reached the office.

Once inside, Dasha retrieved a diagram of the muscles around the eye, looked it over for the twelfth time since Saturday and then went to wash.

As she washed, Preston locked the door and retrieved a thermal pouch from his backpack. He sat on the corner of the desk and prepped the injection, but paused to look at the diagram and then at her. "Are you sure you're okay to do this?"

"I just like to keep a refresher on hand. It's like a security blanket."

His scowl, fleeting though it was, registered with her. He didn't trust her with this, so why had he agreed to it? Having his condition kept quiet was such a big deal?

"Basically, the people you work with or whom you may interact with on a professional level can't know you're human, right?" She probably shouldn't have said that.

"Don't start."

She stepped between his legs and looked at his eyelids, trying not to stare into those ice-blue eyes. "You did the left. Is it fritzing less now?"

Preston's warm, spicy scent hit her, causing her attention to falter.

But, luckily, she knew that her reaction to his scent didn't have to be about attraction. It was about science. Science was blind. Science didn't know about their history. Science didn't take feelings into account.

He only smelled so good because her reptilian brain recognized in him a different pattern of disease immunities than she had, ones that would complement her own and give their offspring a more robust immunity profile.

Not that she wanted to bear his stubborn, perfectionist offspring.

Stupid reptilian brain.

"Dasha!"

She squinted at him, forcing her mind to focus. “You stink,” she grumbled. Lies, lies, lies. “Did you answer me?”

He gave her a look. “If you don’t snap out of it and pay attention, you’re getting nowhere near my eyes with that needle.”

“I’m snapped,” she grunted.

“I said the left has been good, aside from that business during Frist’s surgery.”

Dasha breathed through her mouth. “Is the right feeling funny right now?”

Standing close like this, she could feel heat radiating off him. He heated up the air like a big hunky furnace.

A big hunky furnace with an eye problem. And a god complex, lest she forget. “It looks like there’s a little bunching at the corner. That’s not where I’d anticipated injecting, not part of the closing mechanism.”

“It’s a little tight there but it’s not twitching right now.” He took a breath and laid his hands on his thigh too carefully to resemble relaxation.

“So, you just want the upper lid for now?” Not that she could relax either.

“Yeah, let’s leave alone whatever we can. I don’t want to jump in if I don’t have to.”

Subtext received. "Me either," she assured him, willing herself to ignore the way parts of her body had started to tingle. Parts that remembered how firm and warm he felt, and the way his touch could block out all reason. Parts that remembered the addicting nature of his kisses.

As gently as she could, she prodded the tissue around his eyes. While feeling the muscles, she led him through movements, a quick exam, exploring the delicate tissue until she was certain of her target.

When they agreed, she swabbed the area and picked up the syringe.

Her nerves roared back to life as she lifted the syringe, all trace of her libido fleeing in the wake of fear. "What if you move your head?"

"I won't." His eyes remained closed.

"You don't know that." She stepped back, clearing her throat. "You don't trust me. It might be instinct for you to open your eyes and jerk your head away from a needle coming at them. That sounds very like instinct to me." And her instinct said that she could mess this up and ruin his life. *Again.* What in the world had she been smoking when she'd agreed to do this? Why would she do this to herself?

Because it was safer for her to do it. In theory.

He opened his eyes. "Want me to sit in the chair?" He tilted his head to the desk chair. "I can rest my head against the seatback."

"It swivels! It's a swivel chair! That's even worse!"

Where had that shrill note in her voice come from? She took another step back from him and took inventory of her body. Faster breathing. Shaking hands. The urge to run. Adrenalin could be your friend, until those times it sensed danger when there wasn't any real danger about. Right now, hers shrieked at her like she had a grizzly bear loose in her office.

Run. Run as fast as she could in the opposite direction.

Or just panic and freeze.

Preston watched her, wary as she was.

"Maybe I should do this myself," he drawled.

"No. We could get someone else." She rolled her shoulders.

"No."

"I'm sure your dad would—"

"Dammit, Dasha." His turn to feel nerves.

"I get it, you totally hate him. He's an insufferable, arrogant, controlling perfectionist—but he wouldn't be so hard to deal with if—"

"If you're suggesting that I am the reason he acts the way he does, this conversation is over."

"Let me finish before you turn into a diva out of red M&Ms— I wasn't going to say this was your fault. I was trying to say he must love you a lot to micromanage you and…bug you so much."

"You don't know what you're talking about," Preston said, tension showing in the way he stretched his shoulders.

"I know what it's like to have a father who leaves because he doesn't give a damn. Yours stuck around and continues—"

"He does what he does because he's concerned by how I make him look—that's it," Preston cut her off, the look in his eyes warning her off the subject. "I'm not telling my father about this."

"But you don't trust me. I don't trust me." The problem with warnings…you could only pay attention to them if they seemed more important than what you were being warned away from. And she had a point to make. "I've already ruined your life once, Preston. It's too much pressure!"

Okay, that wasn't exactly the point she'd been going for. Dasha stopped and counted to three. She had steady hands, she could do this. This wasn't really that much pressure. It was a stupid injection. She regularly got up to her elbows in entrails, and this was what she freaked out about? She just needed more sleep.

"You have to lie down." That would stabilize him. "Floor."

He rubbed his eyes with balled fists, the action making him look so much like a lost little boy that her throat constricted.

In the time it took him to settle on the floor, she got everything she needed moved beside him and knelt down.

Awkward positioning wouldn't work for delicate work. Holding the position needed to be effortless so she wouldn't accidentally waver.

She sucked in a breath and swung one leg over his middle to straddle his belly.

"Dasha?"

"Shut up, I'm concentrating." She felt the area again. It felt a little different with his head laid back, but she found her way to the right areas quickly. "Got it. Don't move."

She swapped her gloves for a new pair, rubbed the tips with an alcohol swab and then swabbed the eyelid again as an extra precaution. Just two injections, shallow, close together—everything would be fine.

Holding her breath, she gave them fast, no time to second-guess herself or for her hands to tremble.

Flicking the cap closed on the needle, she dropped it beside his head and placed a gauze pad over the injection area. "Okay?"

"I'm okay," he confirmed, voice tight.

She looked down and noticed he'd splayed his arms out to the sides, like he'd been caught in the middle of making a snow angel. Lying beneath her, he couldn't get as far from her as he had on the walk to the office, but he'd got parts of his body away from her.

Should've noticed that earlier. It instantly cooled her libido.

"Stay still for a bit." She lifted the pad and when she was sure nothing was leaking out climbed off him.

Time to tidy. Try not to think. Tasks could fill up her brain, or at least give her something to focus on besides what she was feeling.

She had known it would be hard to be around Preston. She just hadn't counted on it being this hard. If she were like her mother, she'd be begging pills from the doctor and crying herself to sleep every night.

That's good. Think about that. Preston was like her father. Preston was in that same league—Southern aristocracy, and she was a million generations of poor white trash, just putting on airs. Nothing could ever work with Preston, he wouldn't be able to stay with her any more than her father had her mother. She knew this, she'd just gone a step too far—a step too crazy last time, making sure she couldn't try to make something work with Preston.

Now she could dial down the crazy. Chemistry could be combated. Physical exercise could wipe her mind, or at least leave her too exhausted to even consider what her body wanted to consider.

"Dasha?"

She froze. Could he hear her stupid thoughts? She looked over her shoulder. "Something wrong?"

"Thank…you." The phrase came out broken, like he had to force the words. That didn't make them any less real. It made the splayed arms a little easier to deal with.

"You're welcome." She grabbed a towel to dry her hands and turned to look back at him. They might be able to work together, but he really couldn't be her patient. And he wouldn't be his father's patient. But he needed a doctor.

Right eye closed, Preston remained on the floor, staring at the ceiling.

"You know that thing you didn't want me to start on? I'm starting up again."

Her warning made him look at her.

"You don't want anyone to know. Is there some reason?"

"I don't want to talk about it." Because it sounded lame to him even. He wasn't perfect, he knew that, but his skills were sacrosanct. He couldn't have people knowing; physiological imperfections were harder to defeat than character defects.

"Fine, but you need someone besides me to treat this. I'm not a specialist. I'm kind of a wreck right now too. If you won't see someone in town, then you need to find a doctor out of town to see."

He rose from the floor and moved to sit on the sofa. He couldn't argue with the logic. She was right.

"If it's not cleared up yet, you have to consider the possibility that you need medical intervention more intense than injections. There are surgical procedures."

"I know." He took a breath and then nodded. "I've read all I can find on the condition. You're right, I should find someone."

"Out of town?" she asked.

"Definitely. Know anyone?"

"Not really. But I can find someone quietly. Inquiries for a patient." She stepped over and bent to look at the site. "It's swelling."

"Thought it might." He touched the area lightly.

People would ask. And the chances were good that Davis P. would show up at the hospital today, if he wasn't here already. "Do you need me today?"

She lifted one brow then jumped to irritatingly correct conclusions. "Your dad will be visiting Jason."

"Yes." He stood again and fished around in his backpack. Sunglasses. "Can't wear shades while I'm working."

"No matter how bright your future."

He nodded and swung the backpack back onto his shoulder. "Call me if things get hairy. I'll risk it if I'm going to be sequestered in an OR."

Preston took one last look then left the office. He should really go home, but every minute he spent with Dasha, the softer he became toward her.

Dangerous. It would lull him into a false sense of

security. As it was now, the hunted look in her eyes and the emotion clogging her voice when she'd announced she had ruined his life…he wanted to believe her. She had some good qualities, but getting blinded by them would be a mistake. He hadn't even really recovered yet from making that mistake last time.

The sudden confession about her father also had him thrown. Why hadn't he known that before? And why hadn't he even realized until now that he didn't know anything about her family? He had just always assumed she had the standard two parents, married or divorced but still part of her life. He'd never asked, and she'd never volunteered information.

It probably wasn't the nicest thing in the world to go and pick Frist's brain while he was recovering from his accident, but it would be nice to check on him. Davis P. usually scheduled his surgeries in the morning so it should be safe.

After all, Dasha had told him to make friends on the staff…

Preston rapped lightly on the open door to Frist's hospital room.

Davis P. sat beside the bed, glasses having slid

down to the tip of his nose, reading his tablet. At the knock he looked over the frames at Preston. "Why didn't you come down with Dr. Hardin after the surgery?"

Not big on greetings.

"Too busy." He wasn't lying—he'd been busy trying to weather the storm. He nodded to Jason to redirect the conversation. "How's he doing?"

"The orthopedic surgeon gave him a good prognosis. Providing he gets competent physical therapy, he shouldn't suffer lasting effects to his range of motion or dexterity," Davis P. answered.

Naturally, it was all about the hands. The man had serious abdominal trauma, and Davis P. focused only on how this would affect Frist's career and the likelihood he could still sell his practice to the man he'd hand-selected to pass it on to. The effort it took him to swallow all the negative and childish emotions his father aggravated in him took a few tense seconds.

"I'm glad to hear it," Preston said eventually, and honestly. "So, why are you hanging around?"

"He hasn't fully awakened from his anesthesia yet. He needs to have the situation explained when he's clear-headed," Davis answered.

"Did you cancel your surgeries or office hours today?"

"Delayed."

So he'd left patients waiting so he could come and do this, something far from an emergency. Something that really bothered Preston. "Tell me what he needs to know. I'll stick around and talk to him. I have a free morning."

Davis P. looked surprised, and then dubious.

"I can handle it. Really. And he's my patient."

Grudgingly, his father began to fill Preston in on what the surgeon had said.

Dasha was wrong—his father didn't do any of his micromanaging for him or for Frist. It was about him, what was best for him, what inconvenienced him.

And as much as it bothered him to treat Frist as a case study, the opportunity had presented itself to see just how Davis P. would behave with a son's—or surrogate son's—future career jeopardized by health issues.

So far, it didn't look promising.

For the second day in a row Preston stood at the head of Dasha's parking space, waiting for her to get there.

Groundhog Day. It was October, but Dasha was certain it was Groundhog Day. Any second now, Bill Murray would pop up and throttle an oversize rodent.

"Why are you waiting here?" She wasn't technically at work until she entered the building.

"You didn't tell me what time to arrive. What surgeries do we have this morning?"

"We don't, actually. It's a morning for seeing patients," Dasha said. "There's another trauma surgeon on call so we can perform some general surgeries, like Angie's. Tuesday and Thursday mornings are for follow-up."

"You didn't do any of that last Thursday," Preston said, falling into step beside her.

"Last Thursday was special. You were starting that day and there was a pile-up on I-40. Sometimes office hours get suspended for emergency situations."

She pushed past him in her brisk walk for the building. It had been especially soupy and chilly out this morning. By afternoon it would be far too warm for a jacket, but this morning she would have been happy to be wearing a parka and gloves. Only slight overkill. Her breath fogged the air, for goodness' sake.

And he looked like he was completely at ease in the early-morning yuck.

"So, do you not need me again?" he asked, an edge in his voice.

He'd gone home yesterday because his eye had been swollen and people would ask. It had been to help him. "Well, no. Since the position extended is the same as mine, they want office hours too," Dasha muttered, speaking of the board and expecting him to keep up. She hadn't even had coffee yet. And as confused as her thoughts had been since the kiss—which neither of them seemed inclined to mention—Dasha hadn't realized how much she didn't want him in her space until there he was, clogging it up with his impressive torso and traitorous, beautiful Siberian husky eyes.

"That's fine. You just haven't told me much of what to expect. I'm relegated to following you around and…?"

"Do we have to do this right now?" She unlocked the office door and pushed in, dumping her stuff in a chair so she could dig out some money. Cafeteria. Coffee cart. Now.

"Where do we see the patients? In here?"

"No. This is just Dr. Saunders's office. There is

a clinic style set-up downstairs for different staff to post office hours in."

"Where?"

"I'll show you after—"

"Just tell me. I'll find it." He waved a hand. "You obviously want me out of your presence. Which surprises me as I haven't done anything this morning to irritate you that I can see, and I thought you were all gung ho about saving my career now."

"I am."

"Why is that again?" Preston asked.

"Because I owe you." Dasha repeated the answer she'd given before. It was true.

"No, I mean why now? Why not two years ago? What made you decide now was the time? It's been bothering me. Why now?"

"Can we talk about this later?" Dasha asked, trying to keep the request in a more level tone than she'd used this morning so far. She was having a cranky day.

"Why not now?"

"I can't talk about it right now," she tried again.

"Why?"

"I get upset, okay? And we have patients to see. I can't be seeing patients with puffy red eyes and a tissue in hand."

He watched her for a few seconds, and then nodded. “Okay, but we’re doing this today. Tell me where the clinic is and I’ll meet you there.”

CHAPTER FIVE

PRESTON DID VERY little the entire morning. Probation didn't agree with him on so many levels, but he was determined to see it through. Make the impression they required, and right now that wasn't about what he could bring to the table skillswise, it was more about being able to sit at the table with everyone without giving anyone grief. Or being accused of being hard to work with. Or being called an ass.

He shadowed Dasha, celebrated a fairly significant five-day weight loss with Angie and in general tried to be good. But the instant they were back in Dasha's office, he closed the door and waited.

She took one look at him and started to talk. He liked it that he didn't have to remind her what he wanted. "We've established that I owe you. And you've pointed out my new image a few times, but the thing is I don't think you really understand. Making things right for you is part of what I need to do to clear my books. I screwed you over, and it was probably the worst thing I've ever done. I don't expect you to forgive me. I don't expect your friendship. I don't expect anything from you. I've lived with it, and every day I am in this hospital I think about it. I don't want to live that way anymore. I want to fix it."

"I don't want you to think I don't hear or appreciate what you're saying. I do. And for what it's worth, I believe you sincerely want to make things right." Preston held up his hands. She said talking about this would make her cry, so he had to go gently. "I just need to understand what brought this decision now. Why not six months ago or two years from now?"

"I promised Marjorie I would try to fix this." Not crying yet. Good.

"Dr. Saunders's wife?" Preston prompted.

"Yes."

"Why?"

"Because she's important to me." Dasha didn't want to talk to him about Marjorie. She wanted to help him and move on.

"Why does she care about me? I don't know her."

"She doesn't. She cares about me." Dasha pointed to herself, trying to control the helpless feeling that surfaced every time she thought about Marjorie. It was even worse when she tried to talk about her. Especially with Preston. She may as well spread her innards out on the ground and ask him to run over them with cleats on.

"And she knows about us."

"She said it's a terrible thing to have such big regrets at the…" Stop. No more talking. She couldn't talk about this. She didn't even know if she could speak, her throat burned so hard.

He waited, his eyes on her face. For once she couldn't hold his gaze.

She reached for the water on her desk, wrenched off the lid and wet her parched throat. "She waited too long to make amends."

"And her regrets are what to you? Why are they that important to you?"

"When she was younger, she returned to her hometown for a visit, ran into one of her best friends from high school. But she was in a hurry, and struggling with some things. Anyway, her friend told her she was ill, but Marjorie couldn't let herself have one more worry. She didn't ask what was wrong. Just hugged her friend and told her she was sure everything would work out, and left."

"And her friend died," Preston filled in, when Dasha stopped talking again.

She nodded, and shook her hands out at her sides, as if they were covered with water. "Yes. She needed a friend. She needed to count on her friend." At that point she began gulping in air, her spine so stiff that her whole body shook.

Well, he'd asked for an explanation. Demanded one, really. He just hadn't expected this kind of emotional cascade from Dasha. The harder she fought the tears in her eyes, the more he wanted to wrap his arms around her. Comfort her.

"Did you find any referrals?" Change the subject. Get her talking about something mundane. It was the best he could do.

"Yes." She fished her phone from her pocket and tapped around on the screen. "I didn't know where you'd want to go." She cleared her throat a couple of times, and read off a list of names. "That's one in Memphis, Knoxville and Louisville, and two in Atlanta."

"Referrals by people you know?"

"Yes." She calmed a little, her voice firmed up. "Well, the one in Memphis is a friend-of-a-friend referral. His practice partner's referral. But he's got a good head on his shoulders. If he trusts his friend's referral, I'd trust that enough to check the doctor out for myself. But we can put him at the end of the list if you'd rather."

"Email the list. I'll make an appointment."

She nodded again and concentrated on the small screen. He tried not to watch her, but couldn't keep from checking on her a couple times as she navigated the screen. Her shoulders had relaxed, and she no longer breathed like she was about to founder.

He should probably say something about the talk, but he just didn't know what to say to her. She was suffering. He knew pain when he saw it, and it was written plainly on her face. He couldn't tell if it was for him, or for the friend she was about to lose in Marjorie.

"Sent," she said, and stashed the phone again.

Before she resumed fidgeting—or worse—he leaned away from the door and opened it. "See you tomorrow." A pause and he added, "Don't drive anywhere until you've calmed down."

"Okay," she said.

The door swung shut and he found himself imagining her staring at the door he'd left through, and he wanted to go back again.

Still not immune to her.

Planning on working together and occasionally seeing one another in the halls was starting to feel like a pipe dream.

Something about Dasha made it hard not to think about her. Or everything about her made it hard not to think of her. Even when Preston knew what he was doing to himself by letting Dasha dance through his mind, he still found himself thinking about her. Sometimes without clothes…

That image was hard to dismiss. One thing he could not deny, even to himself: she still turned him on.

He either had to take her to bed or find some other way to get it out of his system.

Preston leaned on the railing outside Dasha's office, coffee in hand, as he watched the slow trickle of morning traffic across the granite lobby, and wished his coffee was whiskey. Still no ideas on how to handle the situation, but her near breakdown had at least convinced him she wasn't up to something that would be to his detriment.

She might still make some bad decision that could effectively gut him, but it was less likely to be premeditated.

He heard keys jangle and looked behind him. "Morning."

"Hey." Dasha looked tired again. Good. Focus on that. Only now he found himself picturing her in bed.

"You wake up late?" Don't flirt.

"Stayed at the Saunderses'. Had only the bare minimum with me. Clothes. Toothbrush. That's about it."

"And did you sleep at all?" He followed her inside.

"Of course I did. Not as much as I wanted, but you make do."

What had he wanted to tell her…? "Atlanta. I need to talk to you about Atlanta. Okay if I take Friday off?"

"Doctor appointment?"

He nodded.

"Absolutely." Dasha resumed whatever she was doing. "Did you get both doctors for Friday?"

"Yes. Morning and afternoon. I'll drive down Thursday evening." And with any luck he'd feel good enough about one of the surgeons to put his sight in the man's hands.

"That's a four-hour drive. Why not fly? It's just a tiny flight."

"Because I don't want to have an episode at

the airport and end up being pushed around in a wheelchair like an invalid." She really didn't get it. "I don't want to put myself into a situation where I have to rely on someone else to take care of me. I'm not helpless."

"I'm not suggesting you're helpless. You're the one that went there with this scenario. I just suggested you fly." She dragged the word out, looking at him again. "But since you brought it up, what if it happens while you're driving down?"

"Then I will pull over and wait until it passes." He answered quickly. "All the roads between here and there have sufficient berm for a car to be parked there."

She grimaced at him. There was no one besides her to accompany him, and the last thing he needed was to be trapped in a car with her for four straight hours. Twice. It was already nearly impossible to get her out of his mind. "It'll be fine."

"It's really none of my business anyway." She shook her head and reached for her tablet. "Sorry. Rounds this morning."

That was his cue. He stood up. "Need anything from me?"

"No, just be your usual charming self."

He grinned. "I'm always nice to patients."

"And mostly nice to the staff. Though you should try to be nice to the nurses without flirting with them." The way she held her chin told him she was upset with him.

That shouldn't please him. "I haven't been doing any flirting. You told me to be nice, and I've been trying to be completely nice."

"Oh." She didn't say anything else right away, but the energetic cleaning of an already clean surface said much.

Jealous. That also shouldn't please him, but it felt good, even if her reasoning was inaccurate. Maybe he'd smiled at the nurse too much. With the reputation he'd built for himself people liked to take things he said in a negative manner if he didn't smile. It was a smile prophylactic. "I'll try not to look flirtatious."

"It was just the one time," she said, shaking her head. "I'm sure I'm just…well, I want to make sure you don't appear unprofessional."

"That one time?"

"With Melody."

The cute one who couldn't be sweeter or blonder if they dipped her in bleach and rolled her in sugar. "Ah. Probably just my reaction to all that sweetness."

She looked at him so sharply he had to smile.

"It's cloying. I prefer some tartness."

"I'll keep that in mind." Dasha ushered him out of the office, hands waving in the air like an exaggerated sleight of hand—trying to wipe away all traces of the conversation from existence.

Methodically, and with Preston at her side, Dasha started at the end of the hall. Not all of the patients on this floor were hers, but she took them one at a time, files organized by room number. Tidy and efficient, just how she liked it.

Preston remained quiet most of the morning. He greeted everyone, shook hands and smiled, but other than that he was more a quiet observer than anything else.

They reached Jason's room and Preston's father was nowhere in sight. Be grateful for small mercies.

"You're awake." Dasha rounded his bed and tucked her hand into Jason's good hand. "I thought you would be in a morphine haze still."

"They took my pump last night," Jason mumbled, but gave her hand a squeeze.

"The jerks," Preston chimed in, smiling.

Dasha looked from one man to the other, holding her breath and hoping Jason could tell joking when he heard it. Preston's manner could take some getting used to. No offense she could see…

Preston leaned against the wall, arms crossing as he looked at the multisplinted neurosurgeon. "I meant to ask you yesterday—what the hell were you doing up that tree to start with?"

"Picking apples."

"You know they sell those at the store these days, man."

Jason smiled then. "That's what I said."

"Picking for a woman?"

"She's making apple butter," Jason said slowly, and casually slid his hand from Dasha's.

Maybe the casual hand squeeze was too personal for a man dating a woman who made apple butter. Dasha stepped back, listening to the men.

Preston shook his head. "She's making it with store-bought apples now, I'd wager."

"I'll remember next time."

They bantered, exchanging jabs in a guy way that she'd normally like to get involved with. Insulting your friends as a method of showing support? A strangely endearing habit she'd picked up from having too many male friends. Marjorie had almost broken her of it.

That realization brought another—they were actually speaking as friends. When had that happened? Good sign, but weird. Had Preston been coming in while she wasn't around, sweet-talking the staff and Not Flirting with blonde nurses?

"I don't mean to interrupt but…mind if I take a look?" She gestured at his side, the area where she'd gone in. Left side. Under the ribs.

"Sure, go ahead," Jason said, and then fell silent. There was an uncomfortable silence from Preston as well as she checked the bandage and went through the requisite steps and questions. "How's your pain?"

"Not bad there. The bone pain trumps everything else."

She nodded. "If you feel like you need something stronger, let me know."

A few taps of her tablet brought up his labs and as she started going over them she was paged. She went to answer and came back quickly. "I need to go to a meeting I was unaware of. Dr. Monroe, you can take a long lunch if you like." She thought for a moment and handed him her tablet. "And can you go over the labs with him?"

"Sure." He stayed seated, but scrolled through the info as she left.

Banter was a good way to make friends, and with the odds stacked against them these two had ground to make up. She wanted to encourage this behavior. And no doubt Jason could use some company.

"How are things going with you here?" Frist asked as Dasha left. "She's a slave driver. Very focused on her career."

"Dasha? Oh, she's not driving me too hard." Preston dropped into the chair beside the bed. "I like to work. Could use something more challenging, though. I'm on trial or something. Have to work with Dasha until the board realizes I'm not going to cause drama."

Frist nodded. There was something else he wanted to say, but was clearly still chewing on it. Preston changed the subject for him. "You want me to give you the rundown on the labs?"

"Anything I need to be aware of?" Frist went with the new subject.

"Your white count is up a bit," Preston said, and then shrugged. "Not too bad. And they are hanging antibiotics already."

Frist nodded again, distracted. "She's kind of fragile right now." He subject-hopped again.

"I know. She told me about Marjorie." Preston laid the tablet in his lap and gave the man his full attention.

"It's coming up on the anniversary of her mom's death too," Frist pointed out.

"I didn't know her mom had passed." She'd told him about her dad leaving, but hadn't mentioned her mother, and he hadn't asked. Again. "How long ago?"

"Long time. She was a kid. But I think this all dredges it back up."

So Frist had either asked these questions or Dasha had shared with him in a way she had never shared with Preston. And that...bothered him more than he'd like. "She doesn't talk about her family much, does she?" Preston shouldn't be so interested in this.

"Well, that's because she doesn't have any family that I'm aware of."

"None?"

Frist shook his head. "She went into foster care when she was ten or eleven."

How the hell could he not know any of this? Because he had never asked, because he hadn't wanted to know. Because he was an idiot and hadn't wanted to know anything that might change their relationship when he'd liked it as it was.

"You all right, Monroe?"

"I'm just surprised." Preston stood up. "We were

pretty close at one point. That's not usually the kind of thing you don't mention to friends." Play it casual. Don't make it weird with this new possible friend.

"Well, you know now. Keep an eye on her if you can," Frist said.

"You look zonked. Need anything before I go?" Preston couldn't commit to watching out for Dasha. He was having a hard enough time watching out for himself right now. Or, hell, watching anything for any predictable amount of time.

"I'm good, man. Thanks."

Preston rounded the bed, heading for the door. "Get some rest." He was going to have to ask her about her mother. It was going to happen. Stupid for him to do, and he knew that… So why in the name of beer and breasts did he keep asking Dasha personal questions?

He made his way into the hall, and then to his car. Find something to eat, get out of the hospital, stop thinking about little orphan Dasha.

He needed to forget that bit fast.

The last thing Dasha wanted to be doing at ten-thirty on a Thursday night? Pulling into an interstate truckstop somewhere in the bowels of Tennessee. But Preston had called.

She'd tried to warn him that it could happen when he was driving, but had he listened? No. Because he was Superman, or just Super-Stubborn Man. Because he couldn't grapple with the idea that he might become incapacitated while on the road, he'd chosen to ignore it.

Now she, white freaking knight that she was, had to spend loads of time with him in the car, and then a hotel setting and then more car time…

At least it was night and she wouldn't have to note the picturesque quality of the Smoky Mountains blanketed with autumn colors. Stupid October.

She maneuvered her car through the tractor trailers and other traffic, looking for Preston's silver Jag. She found him parked in a well-lit area near the combination store and fast-food joint. Well, at least he'd listened to her when she'd told him to do that.

Dasha pulled up beside him and got a peek into his car.

Squint.

He wore an inverted take-out bucket on his head, like some insane paper helmet.

His eyes must be doing that blinking thing, rather than the locking-shut thing he'd told her about happening at Davidson West.

That didn't look at all ridiculous. Though considering where they were, it might be an effective survival tactic. Even hardened criminals tended to give crazy people a wide berth.

She grabbed her keys and purse, and although the area was well lit and she had parked only about ten feet from Preston's car, she wasn't taking any chances. She locked the doors before crossing to his car.

Not wanting to startle him, she tapped lightly on the window.

He pulled the bucket off and eyed her, as well as he could eye her. It only took a couple of seconds to recognize her, and then the window came down.

"Hey, Bucket-Head, you looking for a date?" She winked and flipped her hair. That was as far as Dasha was willing to go in her truck-stop hooker impersonation.

It was far enough to make him smile. "You need a tube top to pull that off."

"A man with a take-out chicken bucket on his head doesn't get to give me wardrobe tips." She reached through the window and tilted the bucket to get a peek inside.

"It's clean. No chicken in there." He shook his head and set it on the passenger seat. The lights must still be bothering him because he pushed his sunglasses closer to his eyes.

"How do you want to do this?" She got back on topic, eager to get back on the road. Safer hurtling down the highway at eighty-five miles per hour…

"There's a tow truck who'll take it home. We'll take your wheels."

"Okay." Dasha opened his door. "Need me to call the tow truck?"

He handed her his phone. "Number's there. Call. I'll move my stuff to your car." He rolled up the window and popped the trunk.

"You call. I'll get the stuff moved over." She could see what she was doing, and as she was currently playing the part of rescuer she may as well be as helpful as she could.

"I'm not an invalid, Dasha. I need a ride, but you don't have to wipe my nose or change my damned diapers."

"Okay. Jeez." She stepped back. "Get it yourself, Dr. Grouchy." She leaned against her car and fiddled with his phone until she found the number he'd directed her to. The urge to snoop through his text messages tickled her sneaky bone but that would be wrong. Ugh. New-and-Improved Dasha would resist temptation. She dialed before Old Dasha made a reappearance. That chick would've snooped for sure. Only way to know he wasn't saying anything bad about her or her trailer-park upbringing.

By the time she'd confirmed the tow and directions to Preston's apartment, he'd moved his bags and was sitting in her passenger seat.

Ever cautious, she made a final check of his car, reassuring herself it was locked up tight, and then returned to her car. He had the bucket. "Do not put that bucket back on your head."

"Headlights are murder."

"Well, I brought you something for that." She fished into the console. "Got my sleep mask."

"You mean those gel things?"

"No…" She snagged it and handed the fuzzy thing over. "It blocks light, and it's loose enough that it won't put pressure on your eyes. They can open and close and not have any adverse effects." And it was a bright cheerful shade of turquoise with a ribbon-wrapped edge—a selling point she didn't focus on. New-and-Improved Dasha still had flaws…

* * *

Preston eyed the mask. It was girly. Not as girly as his stupid gel mask but anything was better than that bucket. He pulled his sunglasses off and slid the mask over his eyes.

Well, it smelled like her. It smelled so much like her it summoned long-suppressed images to his mind—things better forgotten. The feeling of his nose burrowed in her nape, and submersing himself in her scent.

He sighed.

But it blocked out the light. "This is great. Thank you. Good thinking." And thoughtful. He laid his head back and settled down while Dasha got them back on the interstate toward Atlanta.

Ignoring the scent might be as big a task as trying to keep the light from bothering him. At least it didn't hurt. Well, not physically.

"So why did you wait so late to leave?" Dasha asked.

By the vibration of the car and the steady thump-thump-thump of the highway cement seams, he could tell they were back on the route. "I didn't. I left early to miss rush hour. And I waited a couple of hours before calling you."

"You idiot," Dasha grunted.

"Hey, now, no name calling!" Preston laid his head back.

"Well, I told you…"

"Can we spare me the I-told-you-sos?" Preston sighed again. He just wanted to get to the hotel and to bed. Having a bucket on his head for two hours might've been the highlight of his day.

"I'm sorry. I just…" Dasha grumbled. "Never mind."

"What?" If he'd had control of his eyes, he would be rolling them right now.

"I worried."

"Thanks for coming to get me." He tried to ignore the worry comment. The problem was, without being able to look at her, being able to remember all that had gone before them, he didn't doubt for a minute that she did worry about him. He'd heard it, right there in her voice and in the way she'd been griping at him since she'd arrived. Not one to nag, if she felt the need, it was because it meant something to her.

Don't acknowledge it. He shoved it into a big bin of messy emotions to deal with at a later date. "I'm sorry about you having to miss work tomorrow now."

"Oh, it's covered. And I've decided to make the

most of the trip. I have to get a fancy dress of some sort."

"Of what sort?" Talking about something besides him was good. Even if it was talking shopping. "What's the dress for?" He'd never seen her in a dress.

"There are two events; one charity something or other and then there's the winter ball at the Cumberland."

"So, you need a cocktail dress and a ball gown," Preston summarized, losing interest. Cocktail dress could be interesting. Short. Black. Lots of bare leg… The winter ball failed to thrill him. He'd been. Several times. It was lame. She'd hate it.

"Can't I just get one dress and wear it to both?"

He laughed. Dresses were clearly still new to her.

"I'm serious. Why can't I just get one nice dress and wear it twice? You say ball gown and I picture Scarlet O'Hara."

The steady thump of tires over highway seams had a soothing effect, and despite the fact that he was utterly surrounded by her scent and her presence Preston found himself relaxing into the seat.

"You're not far off, but you can probably bypass the hoop skirt if you want. When you go to the shop, tell them you want a little black dress.

You can use that for the charity thing…later on for dinners and stuff. But you'll have to go to some kind of special shop for the ball gown." He paused. "Haven't you ever been to a ball?"

As soon as the words were out, Preston regretted them. Kids in foster care probably didn't get forced to attend balls. And considering that she didn't even know what kind of dress to get… Dumb question.

"I didn't even go to high-school dances. Prom. Homecoming." There was a note to her voice that made him want to see her face. He didn't know quite what that tone meant.

"Come to think of it, I don't think I've ever seen you in a dress." Talk about dresses. Focus on the dresses. Don't ask her about the foster-kid thing. That subject needed to be ignored. It was polite, none of his business. He didn't like it when people pried into his business, so not prying into hers was respectful.

"I don't own a dress or a skirt of any kind. Not counting nightshirts and that sort of thing."

Also don't talk about nightshirts and that sort of thing. "That sort of thing" was probably nightie-related, and therefore a bad idea.

"So you didn't think your new image was for dresses?"

"I didn't know where to begin."

"Ball gown." He chuckled. "Start at the top. Work your way down to miniskirts."

Mmm. Miniskirts. God, the thing over his eyes made it easy to fantasize. Picture things he ought not picture. Women he ought not picture. Woman…

"You've been before, haven't you?"

"The winter ball? Yes. Charity event. My parents dragged me to that a few times," he replied. Silence followed that made him want to lift the eye mask, even if his eyelashes were still fanning the furry interior enough to let him know he shouldn't.

"So…" she started, just as he lifted a hand to reach for the corner of the mask, "you could identify an appropriate dress—gown thing—if you saw one?"

"Uh…" This was starting to sound like a shopping trip forming.

"Please?"

Oh, hell. "Well…"

"I promise not to call you Miss Daisy if you do." Her voice took on a sing-song quality, teasing.

"Sneaky way of getting that insult in there."

She laughed. It was more of a giggle, really. And

had it always been so freaking adorable? "Or I could promise to call you that if you refuse."

"Can't decide on whether to use that jab as carrot or stick?"

"It's all about perspective."

"I guess I can go to a shop with you. You are rescuing me here." A fact Preston would prefer to forget as fast as possible. Wipe that debt out. Even if that meant a day of shopping for dresses with Dasha.

"Yes'm, Miss Daisy."

He didn't need his vision to clamp his hand over her mouth. It was a small car. "Quiet, you."

She giggled again, and her warm breath tickled his palm and passed through his fingers in a way that almost felt tangible. He was getting temporary functional blindness and that heightened other senses. Either that, or he was entirely too turned on by touching her. Preston could feel the curve of her lower lip pressed into the hollow of his palm, and the cupid's bow that rested along the top edge…

He pulled his hand away.

"Fine. Fine."

"I think I'm going to nap." Unconsciousness. It wasn't just for bedrooms anymore.

"What part of Atlanta are we going to?"

"Phone." He fumbled for it where he'd dropped it in the cup holder. "Directions saved there."

"Okay. I'll wake you when we get there."

He nodded and settled his head back. The mask should have made it easy to sleep, but it mostly just made it easy to fantasize. As soon as his eyelids stopped flailing about, he would get rid of the thing. And he'd wash it out in the sink tonight. In case he needed it again on the trip.

Hotel soap was usually pretty pungently floral. Should do the trick. If he could last until then.

CHAPTER SIX

"I'M NOT SAYING you should let a quack take a whack at blinding you with a rusty scalpel."

Dasha groaned, focusing with all her might on how frustrated she was with Preston's doctor-shopping tactics. It helped her keep from focusing on the fact that she was in Preston's hotel room and there was a big comfy-looking bed just right over there. "I'm saying you should at least talk to the man before you decide that he's unqualified."

"Did you see his diploma? Where he went to medical school?" Preston repeated, having pointed that out to her at least five times since they'd left the second doctor of the day that he'd deemed unqualified. This time he said it slower and with more volume than was necessary.

"Maybe he couldn't afford to go to Harvard or Johns Hopkins."

"Poor people go to Harvard all the time. Scholarships exist for that very reason."

"Okay. *Okay.*" No more screaming. This was

about his vision and he had a right to be picky. "It's just that we came all the way down here and you didn't really talk to either of them."

"I know. I was there." He sat on the bed, and then promptly got up and sat in the chair instead. "You're the one who got the referrals. Didn't you ask anything other than a name and phone number?"

"Of course I did."

"For instance…"

"I asked about duration of practice. I asked about reputation and any cases of significance for or against." She paused a second, trying to remember all the things she asked. "I asked whether the one doing the referral would entrust their own care, or that of a loved one, to the physician in question."

Preston rubbed his hand down his face. "Those are good questions, but please start with schooling for any future referrals."

"School only takes you so far. It prepares you, but anyone can make the most of their education."

"Dasha…"

"Preston…" She intoned his name in the same condescending manner he'd said hers. "You have a really crummy résumé, don't you?"

"Do you really want to go down that road with me?"

"Just let me make my point. Someone could look at your credentials and go, oh, good school, and he's got lots of experience, but he changes hospitals every five minutes. He must be defective somehow. And then they would discount a man who is one of the best surgeons in the state, possibly the country. Because miracle worker he may be, he's hard to work with."

"You're not listening."

"I am. I heard you. Next referrals, I'll ask school. For you. Because you need it." She shook her head and tracked halfway to the door before failing to suppress another thought. "Not everyone has boundless opportunities. Some of us have to make the best of what we have to work with." And this wasn't supposed to be about her. It was about a wasted trip and Preston's snobbery. It had just struck a nerve.

"Just for the record," he began, his words coming so calmly and levelly that Dasha stopped another trek for the door to look at him. "I didn't have boundless opportunities. I had two. St. Vincent's and my father's hospital, with fellowships of his choosing. It was an uphill battle to even get to choose my own area of specialty—and then he forced a few more fellowships, trying to change my mind."

Dasha had seen Preston's father and his parenting techniques firsthand the day she'd handcuffed Preston to the bed. "I came back to unlock you. I saw—" What had she seen exactly? "The yelling." The yelling of an overbearing perfectionist who had turned Preston into the neurotic jerk he could sometimes be.

"I know."

So he'd seen her run too, rather than intercede on his behalf and confess her actions. "Right." She really didn't want to talk about this anymore. But it didn't feel like a conversation she could shut down. Penance required the sacrifice of comfort at the very least. "Is there anything you want to say to me about that? I won't be mad."

Hurt? Probably. Most likely. But not angry. He owed her a few truckloads of angry and hurtful words. She was tough. She could take it.

He didn't speak immediately. Like he was picking the perfect words to slaughter her with. "I just want to know one thing."

Dasha nodded, and waited, cramming her hands into her pockets to hide the fisting.

"Did you think you had to do what you did, or did you just really want that fellowship?"

Not what she'd expected him to say. "I never wanted to do that to you."

"That's not what I asked," he said.

"Had to. But that's no excuse. There is no excuse. I know that. I won't ever ask for your forgiveness." She rolled her hands at the wrists, stretching her pockets with the uncomfortable motion. "I'd like to think I'd make different choices if I had it to do over again, but the person I was…the way I'd…" She stopped and swallowed. He didn't know how beaten down she'd felt by life at that point, didn't need to know that for all her practical reasons for having wanted that fellowship, she'd seen him like she'd seen her father—too good for her and built to leave. "I wish I could've been a person who would not have done that to you."

Things had started clicking into place when Frist had mentioned her family situation. An orphan, yes, he could understand how she might feel like she'd had no other options but to be as cutthroat as she required to secure her future. He'd seen kids like that before. The things they'd do for safety and security. And at the time he'd made it clear that he was in a take-no-prisoners mindset for the fellowship. He'd enjoyed competing with her. He'd enjoyed everything with her. He'd even liked the trash talk—of which he'd done a fair amount the night everything had gone down.

And he'd wanted that fellowship. Badly.

Could he forgive but not forget? Maybe. He'd have to think about it. And there were things he needed to know. "There were other trauma fellowships. Why were you so focused on St. Vincent's? Just the prestige?"

"Marjorie," Dasha answered softly.

"What about her?"

"Marjorie was St. Vincent's resident trauma surgeon. I wanted to work with her."

"She was a mentor or something? Someone you knew?"

"She…" Dasha drew a deep breath. "Marjorie was the surgeon who tried to save my mother after her accident." She took a second, and he couldn't tell whether she was wanting him to say something or trying to get something else to come out.

"After the surgery…" She stopped again, and her eyes had gone glassy. She looked away, breaking eye contact with him, and went to tidy the room. "She cried with me."

Those four words knocked the breath out of him. He didn't know what to say. He had an uncomfortable hollow in his chest and felt an intense ache to comfort her, but absolutely no words. Suddenly his reasons for having wanted St. Vincent's seemed paltry and selfish.

"It doesn't change what I did. She was the reason I became a doctor. When I saw the fellowship at St. Vincent's in our last year of residency…it brought everything back and that was all I could see. All I wanted to see." Bed straightened, she turned back to him. Her eyes had dried and her voice had firmed up, but he wasn't sure his voice would be so firm.

A much better reason for wanting the fellowship than his had been. And it had been good for her.

He must have been looking at her strangely, considering his general speechlessness and the way she made for the door again. "I'm going to go to the dress shop. You're off the hook. Rest your eyes."

"Wait." He stood up, shook his head and gestured helplessly. "Are you sure? You don't need help?"

"I'm sure." She nodded, resigned to her shopping fate.

Maybe she needed space. Maybe they both did right now.

"Send me some pictures if you need a second opinion," he offered pathetically.

She nodded again.

"Little black cocktail dress and gown for the winter ball. If you tell them where you're going, someone in the shop will be happy to dress you." He could think about that, so he repeated the advice he'd given her before. Like she'd forgotten.

She took a deep, chest-expanding breath. "Okay. Off I go to play dress-up."

They didn't make a weekend of it. Dasha found nice enough dresses at the first shop she went to, and bought those suckers. Dresses were dresses were dresses. Except for when they were gowns. Whatever. She got them.

Saturday morning dawned and they loaded her car to get on the road.

"Don't put your stuff in the trunk." Dasha opened the door and tilted the seat forward. Backseat. It was tiny, but there was room for overnight bags.

"Why?"

"Dresses in there. If I have to wear them, I don't want them crushed."

"I feel kind of guilty for not coming when I said

I would," Preston said, stashing the bag and flipping his seat back.

She didn't quite know what to say about that. Yesterday had been grouped and filed under the heading "Uncomfortable." She'd prefer not to think about it at all. Truthfully, she didn't even really want him to know that much about her. It left her feeling vulnerable and with the feeling that someone would exploit this weakness.

"Don't worry about it," she murmured, trying to shut it all down. Did she sound as unconvincing to him as she did to herself?

"Let me just get out my woman-speak thesaurus." Preston held his empty hand before him and flipped imaginary pages. "Ah, yes, here it is. Don't worry about it: female equivalent of I'm Fine."

Dasha laughed a little despite herself. "I don't mean it to sound that way. I just mean you don't owe me anything. It's not the end of the world."

"Not the end of the world. Let's check the thesaurus."

"Stop." She groaned the word out. "I'm starting to feel like a talking cliché."

"Do you have an escort?" He dropped his hand.

"Do you mean a date?" She took a quick look at him across the convertible top. What was her face doing? What kind of imaginary thesaurus was he going to whip out now?

"In the loosest sense of the word." He rested his hands on the car top, looking at her over the expanse of black fabric.

"No. I thought about begging Jason to go with me, but it seems he's dating the Home Economics Queen. Plus, there's that whole aspect of being busted up from falling out of a tree and fresh from a few surgeries."

"She's the Apple Butter Queen, not Home Ec—get it right," Preston corrected, grinning at her, but waited until she made eye contact again before he added, "If you can stomach the idea, I'll take you."

"You want to go with me?" *What the...?* "Why?"

"Remember a few minutes ago, that conversation about guilt and debts?"

"Preston, going with me will be unpleasant." His dubious look demanded she convince him. "At best, it will be boring. At worst, soul-crushingly embarrassing."

"You got the hoop skirt, didn't you?" Preston deadpanned.

She laughed again. "I don't know. Maybe. But that's not what I'm talking about. I know nothing about these affairs. I didn't even buy the tickets.

They weren't for me, but they're mine now. They were for Bill and Marjorie. The hospital bought them. I inherited the hospital representative responsibility with the office."

"Somewhere in that I get that you have some meaning that you think I should understand, but I have no idea what you're saying. Who cares who bought the tickets?"

She climbed into the car and waited for him to get in, then started it up and turned out onto the road. "I'm saying I don't know anything about these events, or what I'm supposed to do. I don't know if I'm supposed to hobnob, or if I can wallflower the evening away, as I'd like to. What if they have one of those freaky bachelor auctions like they always have on TV?"

He laughed at her.

"This is *serious.*" She laid emphasis on the last word, trying to drill into him the importance of the possible bachelor auction and other unknown variables.

"Back up, Crazy Train." He was still laughing. "Take your dresses to have them altered. Make a salon appointment for the day of the ball, take the dress with you. Tell them to make you pretty."

She glared at him.

"Tell them to make you prettier." He rolled his eyes. She looked back at the road. "Make you elegant. Then go home, change and I will pick you up. And, because I'm such a stand-up guy, when we're at the ball I'll even make sure you don't fall victim to any nefarious date auctions."

"Will you be nice to everyone?" Dasha asked.

"Probably." Maybe was more like it. Unlikely would've been an even more honest answer.

"Okay." She sighed and then glared at him again. "No dancing."

"You don't dance?" He was not going to spend time teaching her to dance.

"I know the chicken dance."

Okay, maybe he would show her a couple of easy steps at the ball…

"I'm fairly certain they won't be playing the chicken dance there. Unless the class of the ball has dropped significantly since the last time I was forced to go."

"I'm not forcing you!"

"No, every other time I went was under protest. This time I'm signing up."

She sighed and looked back at the road. "All this ball talk is stressing me out."

Dasha kept her eyes on the road, but he could

tell it was harder for her to do the more animated they got.

"Okay, okay. Just follow my instructions, and everything will be fine, Cinderella."

"Men always say that. Charming." She cleared the city limits and said, "Go to sleep or something."

"Am I that dull?" He should sleep. Playing and talking to Dasha felt too nice.

"No, but you paced all night. I heard you. You're tired."

"If you heard me, you were awake too. I'll stay awake and keep you awake." Right, talking to Dasha was now a matter of safety. He adjusted the tilt of his seat a little, getting comfortable, and then started to talk. Work talk—safe, safe work talk. And it was a start.

Maybe more than that. He didn't suspect her motives anymore, but it was more than that. The little she'd shared had changed the atmosphere. A sacrifice of her secrets, hard and painful for her to speak about, but she'd made it anyway. He wanted to tell her it was okay, water under the bridge. He didn't actually know if it was, but he wanted to say it. To talk to her and laugh with her.

To go to bed with her…

* * *

Monday morning, and Preston found himself actually looking forward to work. A change from the way things had been for as long as he could remember. It was a strange contradiction to love what you did and hate going to do it.

He wasn't even sure why it felt different now. Because he was at the hospital he'd always wanted? Could be, but that seemed a bit more childish than he'd like to believe himself. Even though at times maturity didn't stand out as his cardinal attribute.

What had bothered him so much before? The people he'd worked with, for the most part. And while it was a stress-reliever to tell people they were idiots or incompetent—and no one had ever bothered trying to tell him it wasn't the truth—it still tended to make him enemies. And he hadn't cared. Why would you want an incompetent idiot for a friend?

Maybe the staff at St. Vincent's was populated with brighter people? Nah. Not really. It was a great hospital, but aside from him not liking the other ones, they technically had been great hospitals, too. Same caliber. Top-tier facilities. People like Nettle the Arrogant Cardiac Surgeon were everywhere. Dasha had stopped him from calling the man what he was. At least for a while. But she'd shared his opinion. He could say these things to her, and know he wasn't the only one noticing all that was ridiculous around him, and that made it a nonissue.

He stopped by his favorite coffee vendor on the way in and purchased a cup for himself and Dasha, too, just because.

She couldn't always be his confidante, but he wasn't going to mess with a working system before he had to.

Her office door still locked, he took a seat outside it and waited. A few minutes later, his cell beeped. Text.

Running late. Unavoidable emergency. Sorry. One hour.

Emergency. He started to text back, seeking details, and stopped himself. This wasn't a call for help, and him rushing to the rescue would really look pretty lame. Dasha was an adult, she could handle whatever was going on. She'd broken her foot in their first year of residency, and had refused all pain medicine because she'd have had to miss work if she'd taken it. They still hadn't let her operate, but that hadn't kept her from standing in the OR until she'd been kicked out, just so she wouldn't miss out.

She was tough. If she'd wanted his help, she'd have asked. Hounding her as if she couldn't take care of herself was a bigger insult than some social mistake if he was supposed to ask about the emergency.

A walk would be a better use of his time.

Somehow, he found himself outside Frist's room. The man sat in his bed, swaddled in bandages and casts, and hooked to monitoring equipment. No Dasha—so that wasn't the emergency.

He knocked, and dragged Frist's gaze away from the window he'd been staring out of.

"Don't suppose you'd like a double espresso, heavy on the cream…?" Preston lifted a cup in offering.

"And sugar." Frist filled in Dasha's usual coffee order, looking toward the door. "I would. Tell Dasha I begged for it if you have to." He held out his good hand. "The brew here stinks bad."

He didn't seem himself. Or maybe he did. Preston didn't know the man enough to make judgments, but something did seem to be wrong.

Uncomfortable. "She's running late. No coffee for tardy doctors."

"Is she okay?"

At first, Frist's concern for Dasha had made Preston a little uncomfortable, but it was the same with everyone here. They genuinely adored her at St. Vincent's. She hadn't been kidding about the friendliness they fostered among staff. "She seemed okay. Said she would be an hour late." He nodded toward the injured hand, changing the subject. He needed distraction from worrying about her, not to make someone else worry. "How's the recovery coming?"

"Two generations of Monroe concern in one day." His voice went flat. "It's fine."

Preston didn't even have to ask what that meant. Davis P. Monroe had been here already this morning, or called at least. He recognized the signs. "He driving you nuts, too?"

Frist half smiled. "He asks for updates so often, and there are none to give yet. Which—"

"He should know," Preston filled in, nodding. Exactly the reason he avoided telling his father about his own issue. "Well, if it makes you feel any better, I don't really give a damn how your hand is." He grinned.

Frist smirked.

"I'm sure it'll heal as well as any apple-picker needs," Preston added.

Frist laughed then.

"Seriously, try to ignore Davis P. He obviously thinks highly of you." A pause and he added, "You're like the son he never had."

"He has a son." Now Frist looked at him oddly.

"Yes, and you're the son he never had." Preston shrugged past that to joke again. "Let me put it in terms an apple-picker can understand—I'm the bad apple. You're the good apple. Which begs the question: exactly how far did you fall from the tree?"

Frist laughed again. "Not far enough, it looks like."

Yeah, he liked Frist. He knew how to laugh at himself, something Davis P. had never learned. And he provided a strangely timely case study, though he wouldn't have wished this on him. He wouldn't even have wished it on Dasha, back in the day—or a couple of weeks ago. Had his opinion about her shifted so much? Kind of…

No thinking about Dasha. Frist needed a hand right now.

He dragged a pen from his pocket and walked

to a notepad on Frist's table. "My cell number, my home number. These are not for booty calls." He slid the pad toward him. "I should go before we bond over shared Davis P. trauma. But if you need anything—hookers, smokes, apples…" He smiled at Frist, but sobered enough to add, "Or if you just need to talk about anything—" a nod to the bandaged hand "—give me a shout."

Frist looked at the numbers for a long moment, seemed to come to some kind of decision and nodded. "Thanks." He took a drink of the contraband coffee. "We always talk about me."

"Well, we could talk more about Dasha if you like." Preston wasn't really feeling in a sharing mood. This making-a-friend business couldn't happen all at once. He didn't really know what he'd talk about with regard to himself anyway. "She bought a dress. Two, actually."

Frist almost choked on Dasha's espresso. "For real?"

"Winter ball."

"Wow." Frist looked somewhere between horrified and stunned. "I have no idea what to say to that."

"Me neither," Preston confirmed with a shrug.

"Better get back to it." With a wave, he ducked back out.

Half an hour killed, half an hour in which he'd managed not to call and ask what was wrong.

He got his phone out and texted.

You okay?

No phones in the emergency room.

It was coming up on that hour Dasha had promised Preston she'd take, and she'd never once been late to work. Never. She got there early. Sometimes as much as an hour early. Today she was late, and fixing to get later still.

But she didn't want to leave the hospital yet. Marjorie had suffered a fall in the wee hours, and Dasha had jumped and come running at four a.m. when Bill had called. She consoled herself with the fact that she was at the right hospital, even if she wasn't working.

"You have surgery this morning," Bill reminded her as they both trekked alongside Marjorie's bed, en route to her room. She'd been admitted.

"Not for another hour." She turned the phone back on and read Preston's three texts.

"She's okay. You can go to it," Bill assured her.

Nothing was broken, but the tests used to determine she hadn't split her skull in the fall had brought worse news. Metastasis. She'd likely had an absence seizure while standing, and now they'd discovered the cancer had spread to her brain. Spread faster than anticipated. So while she might not have done any damage with the fall, she most certainly was not okay.

"As soon as she's settled into her room," Dasha said, texting "Yes" to Preston. Not true either. But at least he wouldn't wonder if she was in danger. Or dead. Or something.

Twenty minutes later Bill ushered her from the room and she slogged to her office.

Preston sat on the floor by Dasha's office door, reading on his phone. When he heard footsteps he looked up and she nodded to him. "Sorry."

He climbed to his feet and took her bag off her shoulder as she futzed with the office keys. "What happened?"

"Marjorie had a fall."

"She okay?" Dasha opened the door and pushed inside. She looked like she could really do with that caffeine he'd given to Jason. "Did you take her to the hospital?"

"She's been admitted. Probably just overnight." Not making eye contact again. She was hiding something.

"Not the hip, then..." He tried to lead her to the information.

"Head."

"Concussion?"

"Tumors."

Shit.

She'd said Marjorie only had a few months, but if it had metastasized that far, it could be weeks or days.

"I'm sorry." He had no idea what else to say. Again. This was big emotional baggage. He didn't even know how to deal with his own emotional baggage, so how could he help her with hers? No matter how he wanted to. Work. He could help with work. "Do you need me to do anything? Mow the lawn or...take out the garbage?"

"Don't strain yourself." Dasha shook her head at the stupid offers, but moved past it. "I'd like you to take point on this morning's surgery. Maybe the whole day. I don't know. I'll be there, but I know when I'm emotionally compromised. So here's hoping your injections hold through the day."

"I always hope that." He took a seat, more because he had to do something and standing there staring at her would probably only make her nervous.

She started digging through patient files, and was soon briefing him on what was coming in the day.

He listened, although it took effort. Watching her was another story, he couldn't do that. Every now and then her lower lip quivered. He could even see it out of the corner of his eye, and every time he saw it something twisted in his gut.

There were a number of other emotions he'd rather see in her eyes—anger, irritation, even disgust. Anything was better than the glassy look that came and went as she forced herself to keep to her task.

That urge to comfort refused to go. He could blame it on being a doctor, but it still felt like the wrong thing to do. Well, it felt like the right thing, but he made bad decisions when it came to Dasha. He'd resist as long as his will held out.

CHAPTER SEVEN

PRESTON TOOK THE stairs two at a time, hurrying to Dasha's office before she left for the day. Seven long, torturous hours in back-to-back surgeries… and while he'd kept busy, and was busy thanking every divine or fate-adjacent thing that his eyes had not so much as flinched, she'd had nothing to do but stand and stare. Stand and think. Be miserable. He saw it every time he allowed himself to look at her.

It really was lucky he hadn't needed her.

Dasha stood behind her desk when he stepped in, keying in something on her phone with one hand, the other on her bag, ready to bolt.

"Let's go for a run," Preston said, stopping on the other side of her desk.

"I don't feel like it."

"Okay. Basketball." She needed to let off some steam. They were alike in that regard—he abused his body when upset and so did she. Or she used to. It could help if she let it.

"I hate basketball." Dasha shot another idea. But he had more.

"Tennis." Getting her to agree might be a sport in itself.

"Too hard to get a court in the evening." She stepped around the desk, making for the door.

"Country club," he countered, reaching to snag her bag as she walked past again. Though it hadn't worked out so well last time, it seemed like the only way to stop her when she was on the move.

"I don't belong to any country club."

"I do." Hah! Got her.

"I should be with Bill and Marjorie," she mumbled.

"Dasha?"

She looked up at him, those pretty brown eyes dark and hurting.

"You need a break, honey."

"Bill needs a break. He was up earlier than me."

"Maybe Bill just needs to rest and watch her sleep," Preston said, trying to be gentle. "This is their hospital. I guarantee you people have been in and out of Marjorie's room all day."

"But—"

"We'll bring him dinner. Then you're coming

with me." He took her bag off her shoulder so she couldn't escape. "I'll get this for you."

Dasha thought about it. It felt like abandoning them. And what if something bad happened while she was out playing with Preston?

"Marjorie wants you to make things up to me." He read her mind.

That was a dirty ploy. And it worked. "Fine. Basketball in the gym." She could use the exercise. Whatever.

"You said you hated basketball." Preston opened the door for her, and she considered snagging her bag and taking a hint from her name. Dash away.

"I do hate basketball, but we can do it here, now, without driving forever to get to some snobby country club. And I know how to play basketball, even if I find it stupid." Even New-and-Improved Dasha knew she didn't belong in a country club. The winter ball was bad enough, and she was only going to that because of a need to meet expectations. She had to go, even though she wouldn't fit in.

And he didn't need to know about any more of her issues. She'd already hit him with the Mom thing and the Marjorie business. He didn't need to know anything else—the inferiority complex, that she and her mother had been the hobby her father had used to keep his marriage interesting when his wife had been away… None of that. No more talking about her stupid problems.

Most importantly, she really needed to win at something today.

After a quick trip to a nearby deli for something of passable nutrition for Bill, they made it to the downstairs gym and got changed.

Preston didn't waste time talking. Once on the court, he put her through the wringer.

He was fast, strong, clearly had the upper hand and pushed her relentlessly. He taunted her every time she failed to return the ball, ramping up her desire to smash the ball right into his smirking, sweaty face.

Nearing the end of the second game, Preston had to admit that whatever Dasha didn't like about basketball, it wasn't that she was bad at it. She'd finally started to wear down, and it was about time. He was exhausted and his eyes had started feeling funny. But at least the pain he'd seen on her face all day had been replaced by pink cheeks and a fierce scowl. Determination, not defeat.

That offset the realization that he could add exhaustion to his triggers. "You want to call it?"

"No," she shouted, and readied herself for the next play.

Another three points to him before she managed to get one past him. Give her another chance to end it, on an up note. Before he got to ten and she made him play a third game.

"How about now?" He looked at his watch.

"What time is it?"

"Little after ten. They'll probably come to shove us out of here before much longer." He hoped…

A nod answered him, followed by a sigh as she began shuffling to the side of the court to grab her belongings.

He waited. Her feet scuffed the floor—so it wasn't just him who was tired.

With the game over, without having that to focus on, some of the slump returned to her shoulders. Preston stepped closer and wrapped one arm around her shoulders, letting her lean against him. It wasn't really a hug—hugs involved both arms. "You did pretty well. For a girl."

"You smell pretty bad." Dasha made a face at him. "For a girl."

"I'm sure I smell pretty bad for a dude too.

Stench knows no gender discrimination." But he noticed she didn't try to move away from him and his odor. "I like my stench. Brings out my inner caveman. Makes me feel manly. Want to thump my chest and yodel like Tarzan manly."

A short laugh was the most she mustered. She didn't even call him on the stupid yodel comment.

They walked, and Preston realized he was steering her. She lifted her feet and took step after obedient step, mindless locomotion with no intention whatsoever. That unnerved him almost as much as her quivering lip had done.

Make her make a decision. "Want to shower here or at home?"

"Home." But she still let him lead.

He detoured them through some extra corridors to avoid the main areas of the hospital where someone they knew might smell them, and led her to the parking garage. She'd have to make decisions to drive, but he could get her to the car if she wanted to stay blank a little longer. Besides, dark parking garages were dangerous. He was only being chivalrous…

When they reached her car, she opened the door and tossed her bag in, still on autopilot.

"Goodnight, Dasha." He made tracks quickly

before he did something dumb like give her a real hug. Or another kiss.

His departure spawned movement. "Preston?"

He turned around, but didn't walk back.

"Why did you stay with me tonight?" The sadness in her eyes reached for him, like a beacon. It was all he could do to keep his distance.

"I don't know. You looked like you needed some intense distraction." He looked down, fishing his keys from his pocket. "And I know how hard this day has been for you. Thought you could use a little release."

"Oh."

The small sound drew his gaze again. She looked like she wanted to say something else, so he waited.

"Do you want to come home with me?"

That was not what he had expected her to say.

His first thought: *Yes.*

Second thought: *Hell, yes.*

Third thought: *Dammit.*

Fourth thought: *No.*

All further thoughts swarming his head continued to contradict one another. He wanted to. He shouldn't. He really couldn't. Unless maybe that's what she needed? No. No she was too vulnerable right now and he was too wrapped up in her for his own good.

He had to say something out loud. Make a decision. “It’s not a good idea, Dash.”

She tilted her head at him, her eyes almost undoing him. “I have a big shower.”

Ye gods, he wanted to see that shower.

And he knew what it cost her to offer that invitation. Which still didn’t make it a good idea.

Be gentle. Let her down easy, then get out.

He padded back over to her, cupped the back of her head to tug her gently to him and pressed his lips to her forehead. “Not tonight. I’m sorry.” He whispered the words against her skin. “Drive carefully. Eat protein when you get home.”

Probably not the most comforting thing he could’ve said, but there really was no way to turn down such a vulnerable invitation without causing more damage.

Without any further advances, and without even looking at him again, she climbed into the car and buckled in.

Preston stood waiting for her to pull out before he made his way to his car and got in.

An hour later, after one eye cycled through a single eye episode, he went home too.

* * *

At ten minutes before the official start of her shift the following morning, Dasha was still sitting in her car—a safe bubble full of people who loved to shower with her: her. A place she could briefly pretend to be some version of herself from an alternate universe—the one where she hadn't asked Preston to shower with her.

The minutes flew. At five till, the Dasha from this miserable universe—the one who couldn't abide tardiness—dragged herself from the car and into the bubble of mortification waiting outside her window...her very own imaginary hamster ball of humiliation.

Her phone saved her from dwelling further, buzzing in her pocket. Acute care surgeon needed in the ER.

She forwarded the text to Preston with instructions to meet.

Time to save lives. And her sanity, such as it was. If she did nothing else of significance with her life, this would be enough. She locked up and ran for Emergency, her body suddenly reminding her about last night's basketball death match.

Sore. She was sore in new and interesting places today. Muscles that never got involved when she ran now reminded her they existed: hello, deltoids and pectorals.

They both jogged into the department at the same time from different directions. Dasha headed for the nurses' station and the doctor who'd summoned her.

"Big growth," the doctor announced before she could ask. They followed him into the patient's room. A man in his fifties lay on the bed, his shirt open. The lower ribs on his left side pushed at the skin, stretched out of place by something somewhat bigger than a cantaloupe in his abdomen and chest cavity. The ribs must be broken to be at that angle.

Dasha had to mentally kick herself to start moving again. "Sir, who is your treating physician?"

"Don't have one." He stumbled through the words, which spoke volumes about his pain level.

"I see. So you haven't been examined before today?"

"I thought it was gas pains," he said.

Dasha looked at Preston, half afraid he was going to call the man an idiot. Not that he usually called patients names but…

"I'm Dr. Hardin, this is Dr. Preston Monroe. We're surgeons." She checked his chart for his name. "You know we're going to have to get that out of you, Mr. Jackson."

"Will it hurt?" he asked, looking at Preston.

"Yes," Preston answered, "but considering that you're hurting now, the mass is killing you and that you'll be knocked out for the procedure with a steady supply of the good drugs after, I'd say it's a wash on the pain front."

"How dangerous is it to remove?"

"I won't lie to you," Preston said, clearly wanting to lie to the man. "It's most likely going to be a long procedure, and risk factors increase with the duration of surgery. In addition, we can't really tell until we get in there if the growth has attached to any organs. We might have to remove additional organs or parts of them if they have been damaged by the growth. Orthopedic surgeons might also need to realign those ribs, which would have to be another surgery to keep from lengthening this procedure today."

Dasha let him do the talking for now. Men of a certain age tended to prefer male surgeons, and Preston was the best. Her ego didn't need attention.

"How dangerous?" Mr. Jackson asked. "Is it going to kill me?"

Preston thought for a moment and then shook

his head. "It will definitely kill you if we don't remove it. And it will be a painful death, as I'm sure you've already figured out. There's no living with this. Your only chance is surgical."

She didn't know what the man had been thinking, that it would just resolve on its own if he waited long enough? When his ribs had started to bulge, he had to have figured out that it wasn't gas. But she still felt the need to try and comfort him. However meager the comfort, assurances of Preston's skill felt easier to make than to brag about her own.

"I'm sorry I waited. I'm sorry you have to—"

"Don't worry about us, Mr. Jackson. We became doctors to help people," Dasha interjected, reaching out to give his hand a squeeze. Even people who put off dealing with big problems for some unfathomable reason. Or maybe especially those people. She tried not to look at Preston, afraid he'd see what she was thinking written on her face.

They shook hands and she led the way out, instructing the doctor who'd summoned her, "Bring him to OR five. We'll need extra hands."

"Thoughts?" she asked Preston as they hurried for the scrub sinks.

"There's a lot in that area that could be getting damaged even if it's benign."

Or worse, if it was malignant. "I don't understand how it got that bad," Dasha murmured.

"Yes, you do," he said softly. "Fear and denial skip hand in hand through fields of imaginary flowers on a daily basis."

And he probably knew all about that…

Removal of the largest tumor Preston had ever seen firsthand took a little over nine hours.

He'd never opened anyone up to that extent before. They'd ended up cutting through the sternum to expose the chest cavity and continuing the incision down to the navel. And then they'd worked around the tumor, moving in sections.

Spleen near rupture from the weight of the massive growth, cardiac system overworked from the blood required to circulate through the mass and keep it alive. It had taken several people to hold it up so Preston and Dasha could disconnect it from the blood vessels filtering through. That out, they'd moved on to a kidney that had looked too iffy to keep it in there. The lower lobe of the left lung had been similarly smashed and was nonfunctioning.

When they'd made sure it had not infiltrated any other organs, the thing had been fully cut free.

It had taken three people to lift it out, partly due to the positioning required by so many hands in the process and the way they'd had to crowd around both sides of the table, and partly due to weight and slipperiness.

It was a wonder that more hadn't been crushed. For the most part, the growth had shoved things out of the way as it had grown. He'd even give Mr. Jackson pretty good odds of a full recovery. The lab would have to confirm it, but it was most likely noncancerous.

Unlike Marjorie's condition. Unlike the tumors that had invaded her brain.

Preston went for food and coffee, intent on hanging around the hospital until his patient was fully awake and could talk to him about the procedure. And he should check on Dasha.

Actually, he shouldn't, but he would anyway.

Not taking her up on her shower hadn't been about his desires. It had been concern for her. He was way too freaking concerned about her, and yet here he was, with sandwiches and coffee, trying to figure out where the hell she had gone off to.

When he failed to find her at the office or in the

lounge, and discovered Marjorie and Frist had both been released, he gave in and called her.

"Where are you?"

"Radiology."

Downstairs. He hung up. A few minutes later he found her in a dark room, staring at a monitor. MRI. Brain. He didn't even have to look at the patient's name. "You shouldn't be looking at that. She's not your patient."

"You going to report me?"

He slid the food in front of her. "Eat." Then he sat and got started on the slightly stale sandwich while looking at the images.

"How could it get so extensive without us knowing? There are always symptoms to this."

Almost the question asked about Mr. Jackson. Almost the same one he knew she was wondering about him.

Preston pushed the sandwich at her again and looked back at the monitor. Like there was any answer there that would help her.

"Maybe it didn't," he said, when he couldn't come up with an answer.

"You think they knew?"

"I think there were symptoms before yesterday's fall."

She nodded, a weary sigh escaping her. But she'd gotten the sandwich out so he didn't need to knock her down and force cafeteria tuna down her gullet.

"Breast cancer?" He hadn't asked about the diagnosis before. Probably should have. He might have to move on from the hospital if he and Dasha couldn't become entirely comfortable together, but he didn't want to. Staying out of the lives of colleagues had always been a kind of self-preservation, and a tactic he could no longer fully support, even if his instinct still said to keep to himself.

"Yes."

Most common form of cancer in females to metastasize in the brain.

"Before yesterday, had you noticed any absence seizures?"

She paused, chewing her sandwich, squinting slightly. Thinking. "Maybe."

He waited, letting her talk at her own speed.

"She is prone to getting lost in her thoughts a lot. I could have mistaken a *petit mal* for that."

And sometimes those spells didn't last long enough to spot. Especially when you don't want to know. Like Mr. Jackson.

Not like himself. He was fully aware that there was a problem and he wasn't ignoring that. He was dealing with it. Somewhat slower than he'd like to, but he had a plan. And someone to help him with it. God, he needed to find a surgeon.

"I need a ride to Knoxville next week," he said, as there was no getting around it. He couldn't drive himself. He had to have a plan for that too: No chit-chat. No talking about dresses or her past. Their past. His past. The future. Anything. Even if he had convinced himself not to stay out of the lives of colleagues. He couldn't use that plan with Dasha. Not until that's all she was to him: another colleague.

So, no talking except to give directions and indicate the need for bathroom breaks. Leave in the morning, see the doctor, come home afterward. There and back in a day. It was only seven hours in a car with a break in the middle. Not the end of the world.

And definitely no overnight stays in back-to-back rooms with big inviting beds.

Miss Daisy just got more and more demanding every time Dasha drove him anywhere. Today's hardship to bear: no music on the three-hour drive to Knoxville.

Which would be fine if he were willing to talk

to her. But no. No, he got in, thrust directions at her and then promptly got on his own special version of an isolation tank—ear plugs and a sleep mask—and went to sleep. The one time she did try to keep herself awake with some low-volume radio, he woke up, turned it off and went right back to sleep.

Well, if she crashed while zooming up and down these foggy mountains at o'dark-thirty in the morning, it was on him. She'd just have to pass the time poking him in his good eye while they waited for the jaws of life to pry them out. Poke. Poke, poke.

Okay, maybe she was being a little unfair. The text that had preceded her picking him up said he hadn't slept. Or he had, but then his eyes had gone haywire in his sleep and treated him to a special midnight showing of the flicker show. He was probably very tired.

She was tired too, but that was her fault. Her mind had refused to stop spinning round and round the things Preston had said and done the day of Marjorie's fall. And, of course, the weirdness that had come since her ill-received shower invitation.

Her list of people she could talk to about personal issues was largely nonexistent right now. But even though she had a great many casual friends on staff, the family atmosphere wasn't really the right place to talk about this specific problem. Respected surgeons don't go about broadcasting their embarrassment over propositioning a colleague and being turned down.

Marjorie was sick. Jason was injured. Bill was devastated, and rightly focused on the remaining time with the love of his life.

Even if the major players in her life weren't out of commission, Dasha couldn't talk to any of them about that weirdness.

She just had to deal with this on her own.

And maybe find a quilting group, or some other spinster-favored hobby and resume repressing her sexuality.

Dasha waited in the hospital cafeteria while Preston met with the doctor. Snacks. Endless supply of coffee. And it was early enough that the lunch crowd hadn't arrived. She had room to claim a table, spread her stuff out and work.

Less than half an hour into her cafeteria lounging, her phone buzzed. Text.

His fingernails are dirty.

She should be happy he'd at least met this one, but alarm bells sounded. Complaining to let off steam was all right, but preparing his escape hatch was unacceptable. She texted back.

That will scrub away.

Doubt it.

Definitely looking for an escape hatch. How had she become the freaking escape hatch?

Talk to him. Not me.

A few seconds later:

His shoelaces are a mess too.

Panic set in. Not a second scrubbed trip out of town—he was not doing this to her again. A third doctor flushed without a fair hearing.

You'd better stay and talk to him.

Meet @ car.

"Sonofa..." Dasha muttered, and flung a final *NO!* at him. When there was no response after a couple minutes she knew he'd left the office.

Grumbling under her breath, Dasha stashed her phone, gathered up her belongings and hurried to where she'd parked, picturing the ways she could hurt him.

She found him leaning against the trunk, arms crossed

"You are an idiot," Dasha bit out.

"A man who can't tie his shoes properly can't be trusted to operate on my eyes."

She beeped the door locks and got in. He followed, looking as grouchy as she felt. Almost. He hadn't had to stay awake for the trip there.

"You see? And he went to a good school, didn't he? And he still fails at a basic level for you. You're not someone who can be pleased. Ever." She slammed the key into the ignition and started the car.

He leaned his head back, leaving her to guess what he was thinking. "I could do without the lecture, Hardin."

Another thing he'd been doing for the last week: calling her by her last name.

"You should have let me talk to him with you."

"You're just the chauffeur." Preston looked at her then.

"I'm just the help now? Good to know. I know you people can't talk to or befriend the help." She pulled out of the lot. "You can find another chauffeur next time. I've had it, and since we're not friends..."

"I told you at the outset that we weren't going to be friends when this is over." He didn't comment about the ride, probably expecting she'd give in when he asked next time.

"But since then I've been a friend to you. Helping you hide your condition all the time. Driving you all over creation. And you took me to play basketball and offered to escort me to the ball. That sounds like friendship to me." His words had stung. Maybe she didn't deserve his friendship, but he could not lead her on about that. Decide he didn't like her and stick with it rather than this back and forth business.

"That's me paying a debt. Notice I didn't even ask what that second dress you got was for." He turned on the radio.

Dasha gave up talking then. This was because of her shower invitation. Because he wanted her too, or he wouldn't be acting like this. The realization brought little comfort. Things hadn't been this bad after he'd kissed her. And he'd also kissed her head the other night. No matter what he said about duty, he still cleanly sidestepped her references to his friendlike actions to help her deal with feelings when she'd found out about Marjorie's metastases.

If he regretted being kind to her, that was another reason to let him go on thinking she had nothing invested in his probation working out well. Her job was on the line too, but she'd be damned before she told him that.

"You're off the hook as ball escort," Dasha informed him, after chewing on it for several miles.

"No. It's a debt, and I will pay it." Preston tried to shrug her off, turning up the music.

Arguing while driving made it impossible to hit him or bite him. It also made it impossible for him to get away from her. She flipped the radio off.

"Actually, it's not. It's only a debt if it's doing me a favor, and you can be sure that I don't want you there. So it's not a favor. Unless it's your way of punishing me with your presence, you're not going. I'd rather hire a male prostitute and go topless to the stupid ball than take you with me."

"Don't be so freaking dramatic." He didn't turn

the music back on, but she could tell he was thinking about it.

"I'm not. I'm being practical. I'd rather go alone." She was successful, independent and she didn't need an escort.

"Do not ask Jason." He enunciated every word.

Jason? He got a first name now, and she didn't? "Wouldn't dream of it. He's injured. And with someone."

"It's settled, then. Consider it a work function. I'll take you," Preston announced, like Tyrant of the Winter Ball. The king of the ball would have had some manners.

"I have the ticket so I get some say in who I take with me."

"I'm going to sleep. Let me know when you come to your senses. Or when we get home. I imagine the latter will happen first."

Jerk.

He laid his head back and closed his eyes, once again cutting her off to make the drive alone.

Only now she was actually glad.

She turned the radio back on. And turned it up.

CHAPTER EIGHT

PRESTON PULLED HIS Jag into the wide cement driveway of Jason Frist's new two-story brick home on Nashville's west side. A true first for him—Preston had never visited a colleague at home when there wasn't a party going on and other people to blend into. And even then that had only happened a couple of times.

A tiny blonde hottie answered the door. "Jason is in the living room, resting."

"Asleep?" He stepped inside, stopping so she could answer before he accidentally woke Jason.

"Oh, no. In the recliner. Just this way." She gestured him to follow and then disappeared into the kitchen.

Jason greeted him with a wave and motioned to an empty seat.

"Apple Butter?" Preston mouthed the question as he sat.

Jason nodded.

She picked right then to return with a tall glass

of sweet tea for him. "Thank you," he said, and when she'd gone again he murmured, "Think I'm starting to understand why you got up that tree." He'd done dumber things in the cause of wooing a woman. He'd certainly made dumber decisions with Dasha. Choosing not to probe into her past to avoid confrontation hadn't worked out as he'd intended at all.

"Yeah. Doesn't need much explanation," Jason agreed with a rueful shake of his head. "I tried to call you yesterday."

"Oh? Sorry about that. My cell coverage was spotty. Had a day trip to Knoxville," Preston explained. Sort of.

"Knoxville?" That made Jason's brows lift. "Funnily enough, Dasha went to Knoxville yesterday too."

"She told you about that?"

"She called to check on me last night. It came up. But not why." Jason watched him closely.

"Ah." One of the perks of not having friends was not caring how they felt about stuff you did. Now he found himself caring and uncertain how to handle that. He'd come to talk about Dasha, but not yet. He needed to work up to a request—he never asked favors, and this required finesse. If Frist really was a friend to both of them, he would accept. At least Preston hoped so. Until he got around to it, he changed the subject. "How's it going with Davis P.?"

"Same."

"Want me to tell him to back off?" That's how he'd like this favor business to go down. He'd handle Davis P. for Jason, and Jason could handle Dasha.

"Not yet."

Damn.

Jason took a deep breath, and when he breathed back out again seemed over whatever tension Preston's father roused in him. "Why do you always call him Davis P.?"

"He's always announced his middle initial when meeting someone. No other Davis Monroes lousing up the area, let alone Dr. Davis Monroes, but he still adds it. Always bugged me." Preston shrugged. Him shining a light on it was something that had bothered his father when Preston had been younger, angry and actively trying to make the old man miserable. But now… "It's a habit, I guess. Started out as a way to note his ego, but now it just kind of feels weird to call him anything else."

"What's the P stand for?"

Preston grinned. "Preston."

"Lucky you."

"Indeed."

"You could just call him Dad," Jason suggested casually.

"I think he'd have a heart attack if I did."

Jason laughed. "Maybe. Not that I want to dissuade you from visiting, but do you have something on your mind?"

"Yes. I need to engage my lameness," Preston said, because he didn't like feeling protective of Dasha. He'd rather rag on himself over it.

"Pardon?"

Rag on himself and make no sense to Jason… "Did Dasha tell you about Saunders's wife?" Preston tried something more direct.

"Yes," Jason confirmed.

"Good. She needs someone to talk to," Preston said, still working up to the favor.

"Someone besides you?"

And there it was.

"Yes." Preston laughed, a short, hollow sound. "We're in a difficult patch right now. But she's hard to hold at a distance, even when I'm bothered and trying."

"I see. I won't ask what the problem is between

you two—I know there's a history there. But, man, maybe you're not supposed to hold her at a distance." Jason smiled at Apple Butter when he saw her through the open archways.

"I've thought about that too." Preston looked toward the woman and back to Jason. "It's the timing." He took a long drink of his tea, his mouth like sawdust. It got that way when he thought deep thoughts about Dasha. "Will you call her up and check on her?"

"I'll try, but she might not want to talk to me about this stuff."

Preston had said his piece, now to do with Jason what he'd failed to do with Dasha: ask about his life. Starting with Apple Butter's real name.

"So, a cyclops goes to the doctor and says, 'Doc, you gotta help me. I can only see out of one eye.'" Preston hadn't been doing much joking in more than a week, since their return from Knoxville. And he picked today to joke around with her.

Dasha looked up from the notepad before her, tracking Preston's path into the office. He closed the door behind him and removed his glasses. The left eye was shut, like he'd gotten caught mid-wink and his face had frozen that way.

The other eye narrowed when he saw her face.

"What's the punch line?" Dasha asked woodenly. It was the kind of social cue she could figure out right now. Knock-knock. Who's there? An easy pattern to establish.

"Still working on that," he said, but didn't say anything else yet. Staring apparently took too much of his concentration.

Or maybe he was just thrown by the fact that he was joking with her. Every hour of the last ten days had been strictly business. Work, no socializing.

"If you're looking for joke help, you've come to the wrong place," Dasha murmured.

"What's wrong?" he asked, not moving from where he stood on the other side of the desk, watching her.

"Nothing. Everything." She shook her head. Talking about it was another bad idea. Besides, he'd asked Jason to talk to her—like he was shopping for a therapist for her. "I have to leave early today. Which is good for you, considering your eye situation."

"Surgeries?"

"Nothing scheduled. It's all general surgery rollover. I already got another surgeon to come in. You can go home. Or you can stay and shadow him if you want to try it." She stood up and stuffed her tablet into her bag.

It had been packed for thirty-seven minutes.

Thirty-eight minutes ago Bill's brother had called to tell her Marjorie had passed away.

Nothing. She felt nothing. She should feel something, but she'd felt more the last time she'd lost a patient.

Preston nodded, not confirming what his plans were. He still stared. That should probably bother her.

"If you decide to go home, wait until it's safe for you to drive. Hope it feels better soon."

"Dash?"

"Hmm?" She looked back, pausing with one hand on the door. He did look fairly silly with that endless wink, but joking about it was something only a friend could do.

"What's wrong?" He repeated his earlier question.

"I'm late." She didn't want to tell him. She didn't want to say the words. Maybe that was some kind of feeling. And, besides, saying the words might be like knocking over the first domino. Numbness was preferable to breaking into a million pieces.

She left him looking bewildered and drove to the

funeral home. Bill needed help making decisions. It was the sort of thing a daughter would do. Even a pretend daughter.

At half past nine Dasha pulled into her driveway and found Preston's Jag waiting, the man leaning against the front tire well, arms crossed.

She opened the garage door and drove past him, but left the garage door up long enough for him to walk in behind her. By rote, she locked the car and unlocked the house. Once inside, she spoke. "What are you doing here?"

"Jason told me."

She closed the door and wandered through the kitchen to the rest of her modest little cottage, leaving him to follow. "The service is tomorrow afternoon. They have family driving down tonight."

"Far to travel?" he asked, like someone who didn't know what else to ask. But they'd never been big on talking. He'd never asked questions, and she'd got the message loud and clear: he never wanted to know. Why that was different now *she* didn't want to know.

"Some." Small talk was stupid. She put her things on the dining-room table and kicked off her shoes as she walked on. Even tidying had lost its appeal right now. "I'm tired. It's late. Say what you came to say so I can go to bed."

"I didn't really prepare a speech."

"Wing it." She slumped onto the arm of the couch and waited. Strange to see him in her house. His eye looked better at least. So he could see her house and compare them. His home probably reeked of glass and chrome, with a disco ball and a hot tub, and those fancy colored lights that swirled the stage at the Wild Horse Saloon—it was just around the corner from his apartment. Standard equipment in that area.

Her house had no particular style. Just comfort. Everything in the wee cottage had been selected for the emotion it provided. Comfort. Beauty. Warmth. But nothing looked all that comforting right now.

"I'm not leaving," he said, drawing her wandering attention back to him.

"Hmm?"

"Tonight."

"You're not leaving here?" She put the words together. It didn't help her understand.

"I've decided I should stay tonight."

Dasha rubbed her head. Fighting with him seemed like entirely too much effort. He wanted to sleep over. "Okay. There's probably something to eat in the fridge. I'll get you bedding for the couch." She slid off the arm of the couch and started for the hall.

"No." He closed the distance between them but didn't actually touch her. "Just wait a little bit."

"I would prefer solitude right now." It was less confusing, and there was nothing about this current situation that wasn't confusing. Not that she had the will to point out to him how he flipped between telling her they weren't friends and acting like a friend. Back and forth, back and forth.

"Just sit with me for a little while first," Preston said.

"Why?"

"I need to know you're okay." If someone could shrug verbally, Preston did it. He didn't want to be there, and yet there he was.

Another contradiction she didn't call him on. It could wait for another day. "Can you be quiet?" she asked.

He smiled a little then. "Better than you."

Dasha gave in and rounded the couch again. The lights were still off, the television sat silent and so did she, right in the middle of the couch. She'd sat with him when he'd needed someone. These messy feelings could be sorted out later. Some time after tomorrow. Tomorrow was bound to be as messy as today.

Preston sat by the arm. For a minute or two they sat together, silent, not touching. And he'd seen nothing so far to convince him that she was okay.

Silence was hard. He struggled not to say something. But the something would no doubt be even more lame than platitudes. Offers to take out the trash or mow the lawn.

Sitting still was hard too. Not touching her. There his will failed him. His will didn't give a damn about logic right now. She hurt, and he didn't want her to hurt.

He reached over to take her hand, much as she had done for him in the dark in her office. But he couldn't maintain the distance. He slid closer and pulled her hand into his lap so he could hold it in both of his. So small and soft, and as fragile as she seemed to him in that minute.

He had to make some kind of decision about what he could give her. Grieving over Marjorie's death wasn't the sort of thing he could make her wait to do until he'd figured out what the future of his vision and his practice was. She needed someone now. Even someone who couldn't think of anything useful to say to her.

In his life, any time Preston had been confronted with unpleasant, gut-twisting emotions, the best words he'd been able to muster had been sarcastic, a kind of gallows humor to let someone else know that he felt bad too. A defense mechanism. He was self-aware enough to know what it was, but that didn't mean he was self-aware enough to embrace pain, examine it, and whatever else he was supposed to do to make it stop. Words couldn't make bad things go away.

But maybe that's why she'd never shared those painful parts of her life with him when they'd been together.

"You can talk to me, if you want to," he offered eventually, as unable to keep quiet as she had been. "We can be friends tonight, and let tomorrow sort itself out. I'd like it if you would talk to me."

He let himself look at her face, at the tears bending her lower lashes.

She wanted to say no, and that should make him feel better—if she was as wary as he was of getting too involved, that was a good sign they could make everything right again later. Fear and pain warred in those beautiful brown eyes.

He'd never actually seen someone's walls collapse before. She didn't talk, but great ragged breaths escaped her as she suddenly crawled into his lap and buried her face in the side of his neck.

The shock of it made it hard to breathe. She was crying. *Dasha* was crying. Not talking. Crying… real shoulder-shaking crying.

He had no words for this. It scared him in some way he couldn't name.

Wrapping his arms around her, Preston did the only thing he could think of and rocked, burying his nose in her hair. When she cried harder, he held her tighter.

By the time she stopped, his arms ached almost as much as his chest did.

It took the slow fan of her breath on his wet shoulder to confirm that she'd fallen asleep. He'd never been so happy to have someone sleep on him. He closed his eyes and tried to relax as best he could without letting go of her.

He couldn't sleep like this, but nothing in heaven or hell could make him wake her right now.

When his legs started to fall asleep, he slid off the couch, one arm under her knees and the other across her back, and crept to the bedroom.

Small house, so he wouldn't have far to go to

reach a bed. He went for the door at the end of the hall. Bedroom.

After he'd laid her on the bed, he pulled her shoes off. This was a new experience. Old Dasha would never have let herself fall asleep in his arms. Not until they had already spent themselves in sweaty bedroom hours and their choice had been sleep or pass out.

She'd likely be mad if he undressed her, but anger he could deal with. He eased her scrub pants off, left everything else in place and got her under the blankets. A few minutes later, in his boxers, he joined her.

Funeral tomorrow, so he'd have to extend this friendship…thing. After that, he could try to distance himself again. Two days, then he'd stop it. Go back to…whatever they had been doing before.

Trying to put the whole thing from his mind, he turned off the light and settled against her.

He absolutely couldn't make good decisions when it came to this woman.

The smell of sandalwood teased Dasha from sleep. She inhaled slowly, that first tickle of consciousness rousing her from sleep. Preston always smelled just a tiny bit like sandalwood. Her other senses caught up slowly. The heat of him at her back. The comforting weight of his arm draped over her. The soft fan of his breath in her hair.

Still asleep. He really could be quiet better than she could. She had no memory of going to bed. Just the steady thump of his jugular against the tip of her nose, the warmth of sandalwood every time she breathed in, then morning.

Slowly, she shifted onto her back so she could look at his face. No trace of his frequent ego flares in the brows in sleep. No frowns or scowls, and every bit as handsome—even without the brooding looks or occasional playful light in his eyes she'd grown to like so much.

She really missed this. After their uneasy alliance ended, she should make a concerted effort to find someone she could share this with. To hell with the spinster hobbies. After the end, after she'd fixed her mistakes, maybe she could forgive herself and relax about other people finding worth in her. Marjorie had found her worthy. Bill. Jason.

The arm draped over her tightened, tugging her more firmly to him. Now, however, her body didn't conform to his. No spooning could take place with the little spoon on her back.

The wrongness registered with him. She saw it

first in the frown line that appeared between his dark brows. From there, it spread over his features, until his mouth firmed and the jaw—now covered by a growth of black stubble—flexed.

His eyes opened, icy blue surrounded by a dark blue band. Truly remarkable eyes. "You're awake."

"Yes," Dasha murmured. "And now so are you."

He lifted his head to see the alarm clock. "Eight. What time—?"

"It's in the afternoon. For the travelers," she answered, then tried to wipe it all from her mind. She wasn't really ready to think about that yet.

"We should probably get up." He laid his head back down and closed his eyes, lip service paid to getting out of bed. Rather than try to pull her against him again, his hand sought the bare skin of her hip and strong fingers splayed and caressed. "How are you?"

How was she? Dasha had no idea. He'd never asked that question before. But she knew how he was. Groggy. Adorable and groggy.

"I'm okay." She answered on autopilot then found the words to be true. She was okay. Better than yesterday. Better than…any day since Marjorie had been diagnosed. Peace. She felt peace. She was still sad, but the darkness had lifted.

"Do you believe in God, Preston?" He'd wanted to talk…

"Mmm…" He frowned a little more but didn't open his eyes. "I don't know if I believe in the Sunday school version, but I do believe in something that ties us all together. I like the idea of the soul being a spark of the divine, and at the end returning to the source."

Dasha smiled a little at his still-closed eyes and noncommittal Preston-like answer. She was about to screw things up. "I lied to you."

He opened his eyes.

"Well, not lied, but I've changed my mind about it."

"What?"

"I want your forgiveness," she said simply. And she didn't even feel guilty for admitting it anymore. "I said I'd never ask for it, but I have to ask for it. You don't have to give it, and you don't have to make any decision about it right now. But I want it. If you try it on and find it will never fit, I'll understand. I know that is a real possibility, but I still want it."

Preston looked at Dasha as she spoke. Was this a side effect of the looming funeral? God talk and now forgiveness? He'd asked her to talk…

He'd just thought the talking would involve her telling him how she felt and him saying he was sorry and the other things people said when a loved one died. But this was real talk…and about something he didn't feel able to make a decision about right now.

The fact that she was hurting coupled with his need to help her meant he was inclined to give whatever she needed. But if it wasn't real, if he didn't know for sure…he might take that forgiveness back later if everything fell apart. If his eyes couldn't be managed, if his career was over, he'd resent her even more. It seemed more cruel to give something, let her get used to him being around, and then take it all away again.

"I don't have an answer right now."

"Okay." She smiled, tired though it was. The sleepy softness had started to fade from her eyes. Still sad, but bearing up surprisingly well. Better than he'd expected. Better than he could have pictured last night.

The memory of her soft and shaking in his arms brought its own kind of vulnerability, something he hadn't planned for.

She looked at the clock, giving him the privacy

of not reading all this in his eyes. "I really don't want to go to the funeral. I'm awful."

"No one ever wants to go to a funeral."

"Have you ever lost anyone close?" Dasha tilted her head to look at him again.

Just you.

"No."

"Where's your mom?"

"Boca," he answered, watching her in return. Her face had changed a little since the last time they'd lain in bed together, but her beauty had only grown. Now, with different hair and no insane earrings or jewelry that had always looked like she'd lost some kind of bet… No longer trying, she was beautiful.

"Do you get along?"

"Yes. I love my mom," he assured her. She'd lost her mom. Her dad had left. "Do you ever see your father?"

"Not since I was little. When…when Mom died… they asked…you know, the court people wanted to know who he was but as Mom never put him on my birth certificate, I wouldn't tell them."

"Why not? He could have had family…"

"He left us. He didn't deserve to know about her, and I…didn't want to face the idea that he might not have cared. It was better to picture him finding out later and suffering for it. Which I'm sure never happened." She took a deep breath. "He was married, and only came around when his wife was out of town."

"It wasn't Davis P., was it?" he asked, smiling at her in the hope she could see he was teasing. "My perfect father cheated on Mom with Future-Wife-Number-Two, so she left him."

"How old were you?"

"Sixteen."

"Did you live with her?" Dasha asked the questions with an ease he wanted to feel.

"No. She left Tennessee immediately."

"You could have gone with her," she said.

"But then I couldn't have punished my father for hurting her." He wanted her in his arms again. Casually, he reached for her and slid an arm beneath her head, keeping her close. "Too hard to make Wife-Number-Two miserable from hundreds of miles away."

She laughed. A short, weak laugh, but real.

"I can only imagine what that was like."

"I doubt it. I was a monster."

"So it's a long-standing pattern," she teased him.

The light returning to her eyes brought him a

special kind of relieved misery he was happy to stuff behind some sarcasm and humor. “Brat.”

Without warning, she slipped from his arms and stood. The simple cotton bikinis she wore clung perfectly to her bottom.

He looked away. It would be so easy to pretend everything was all right between them. Drag her back to bed. Do all kinds of things to each other…

Her scrub top landed on the bed.

He shouldn’t look.

Her bra landed atop it.

He looked.

Good God, he looked.

She watched him, and when she was certain she had his undivided attention, down came the panties. He stared. Paralyzed with thoughts.

So well groomed.

Running was superb exercise.

Those perfect breasts…still perfect.

“I’m going to shower,” she said.

He blinked and had to really work to make his eyes refocus on her face.

“I’ll be leaving the door unlocked.” The vulnerability that had come with the last invitation was gone. It wouldn’t kill her if he said no. But it might kill him.

* * *

Ignoring the issue of forgiveness—she still needed comfort. That was the primary reason for his visit. Comfort. And things were already messy in this window where things didn't count…until she got okay after the funeral. If they could go back to whatever they'd been before she'd cried, sex wouldn't make that harder…

He watched her cross to the master bath and with the closing door, his own walls fell. Consequences be damned. She needed this. He needed this…he deserved it. Maybe it would be good. Closure. A way to say goodbye, a way he'd never found in trying to just forget her.

No, don't think about that. They were being friends for a little while, not thinking about ghosts from the past. Right now she needed him, and… he needed her too.

The sound of the shower drew him to the bathroom, stripping as he went.

Tomorrow. That was always the plan.

They'd go back to the problems tomorrow.

Or in a few days.

Dasha adjusted the water, finding a good temperature just as Preston barreled into the room.

Thank goodness. If getting naked had failed, she'd have had to enter therapy to keep from developing a complex. Or spend more time at the gym. With a personal trainer.

"This doesn't mean anything." The words came in a rush as he grabbed the condom she'd set on the counter and wrapped his other arm around her waist to pull her to him.

"This doesn't mean anything," she echoed, both arms rounding his shoulders. Her hands, still wet from adjusting the water temperature, glided over firm, tight skin. Marvelous shoulders. Marvelous arms…

His head came down, silk and scrape with his hot mouth and the stubbled cheek against hers. She might have beard burn after this, but it didn't matter. For the first time in a long time her body vibrated with sensation, hyperaware of every place he touched her.

Crisp manly hair tickled her belly where flesh melded together.

Long and strong, his fingers splayed over one cheek, squeezing and kneading the plump mound of flesh in a way that expressed his appreciation more honestly than words could ever have done.

In that moment, he didn't care about the things

she'd done and she knew it. It gave her a glimpse of how good it could be to be wanted by this man, to be cherished by this man—which she felt in the length of his erection wedged between her legs, pressing along the heated seam of her sex. She even somehow felt it in the scrape of foil wrapper grasped by the hand at her back.

The last time she'd successfully had sex with a man had been with this man. This glorious, beautiful, infuriating man. She wouldn't fool herself into thinking she'd been his last too, but the urgency in his kisses, the thrust of his tongue into her mouth, the demand in his touch and the way he backed her into the spray told her he needed this as much as she did. In that moment they were equals.

A little voice in the back of her mind said this was wrong. The same voice that stopped her every time she tried to get close to another man. The voice that had always won.

This was wrong.

She was using him to feel better.

He would want any other woman just as much in that moment.

But he knew everything. Or he knew enough. He knew what she was feeling, why she needed him so sharply in that moment. It couldn't be using if he knew.

His tongue in her mouth, the water cascading over their entwined bodies, the silken strands of his black hair between her fingers…all spoke louder than that small voice. For once.

Firm and insistent, his erection nudged at her belly—he continued backing her into the shower, until the little toiletry shelf pressed into her back.

His hands curled under her cheeks and he lifted her until she sat on the edge of that precarious little shelf.

That did give the little evil voice some power. She could fall. Get hurt.

One of her hands left the muscle-corded shoulders and flailed at the shower wall until it found a safety bar and gripped it for stability.

Without ever breaking the kiss, he had the condom out, on and pushed slowly into her.

Dasha locked her legs around him. Stretched. Filled. Chained to him in a way that felt…something. Recognition?

Ridiculous. Bodies didn't remember. Minds did. Hearts did, metaphorically at least. But this was just muscle memory. It didn't mean anything…

He started to move, and five long lonely years

melted away. She found his rhythm, and as much as she could, moved to meet him. But fear made her clumsy.

"I'm going to fall," she panted into his kisses. "Maybe we should move. Rug. Change position..."

A groan tore out of her as a warning tremor shook her, obliterating what she'd been trying to say.

"Fall." She panted the word again, gripping him and the safety bar with equal fervor.

"You won't fall," he promised, sealing the words with more intoxicating kisses.

Her hand slipped on the bar. "I don't want to fall." In the steamy shower, her words sounded louder, more desperate as they bounced off the tile surfaces. More than real. Prophetic. He would drop her. She would fall if she didn't hold on.

"Dasha." He said her name and stopped moving until she looked at him. "Let go. I won't let you fall."

He couldn't know that. People made mistakes. They made bad decisions. They failed those they cared most about, and she was, what? Not even his friend most of the time. For the next few minutes only she was his lover. That was it.

"Trust me." He flexed his hips against her, one

flesh for now. One temporary flesh. Her heart squeezed and stuttered.

He couldn't trust her if she didn't show trust in him. At least in this she could trust him. Maybe not the future, maybe nothing else could ever happen between them, but she could pretend and trust him now.

She peeled her fingers free of the bar and immediately wrapped her arm back around his shoulders.

With that one simple act of surrender the pleasure Dasha had denied herself for years shattered her. A flood of sensation sucked her under and rippled through every muscle. He was almost there, she could feel it in the jerky way he'd begun to move, and his ragged panting.

Dasha pulled her arms from his shoulders, sliding her hands to cup each cheek and hold his gaze, letting him see every lingering spasm of her orgasm.

Inside her body—inside her eyes—Preston's pleasure crested hard and fast. As the last waves of climax faded he felt his strength drain and leaned into her, using his weight to keep her from falling and to keep his promise. He wasn't ready to leave her body.

This should feel wrong. He rested his chin on her shoulder, soaking in the feeling of being wrapped up in her. Peace washed over him.

Probably another instance when he should say something—but that would mean he had to analyze the act and how it would linger when they had to return to the real world. Not something he was keen to do.

As if sensing the turmoil rising within him, growing even as his heart and breathing slowed, Dasha combed her fingers through his hair and whispered, "This doesn't mean anything."

Words that were meant to free him—or her. He couldn't tell.

The peace faded.

With effort, he slipped out of her, and then lifted her from the shelf edge. As soon as she stood safely on her own, he let go and handed her the shampoo. Showering still needed to happen.

This didn't mean anything.

CHAPTER NINE

BILL'S TEMPORARY REPLACEMENT couldn't take off time too, especially not for the same reason the real head had taken leave. Hospitals didn't cease to operate or be busy just because someone experienced loss. Better Dasha deal with everything than Bill.

Preston had called after the service to check in, and then not again. The prospect of seeing him worried her slightly.

Physical reminders of their shower had faded, but the emotional ones were still going strong—hunger being the most demanding reminder. She wanted more. She wanted him, as stupid as that was. She wanted him in a way she now found supremely difficult to ignore.

But she had to. Ignoring it was the only way to move forward. Taking comfort in the discovery that she did still enjoy and want sex. She wasn't broken.

Maybe she just didn't find men who didn't antagonize her sexy.

* * *

Preston's eyes were getting worse. The injections could only be given on a highly regimented schedule, but the effects of the dose failed to last as long as the necessary interval between.

Add to that the fact that stress was one of his triggers, along with the prospect of several hours of discomfort over a dead turkey, and you had the recipe for a Thanksgiving Disaster.

Or what was commonly just called by the shorter version: Thanksgiving.

No way would he get away with wearing sunglasses for dinner.

He briefly considered texting Dasha the suggestion that she should call him in for some kind of dire emergency—believable when considering how unseasonably treacherous the weather had turned—but things were already hard enough between them without relying on her further. His first reaction to anything couldn't continue to be about Dasha, how she felt or how she made him feel.

He tilted his head back and applied some eye drops to counteract the dryness that now regularly plagued him. When the evidence was gone, he opened the door, grabbed the pumpkin pie he'd bought at the best pie place in Nashville and headed for the front door.

Eat fast. Fall asleep watching football. Pray Dasha summoned him. That was an acceptable plan.

Wife-Number-Three answered the door.

"Sandra." He held the pie box out.

"Thank you, Preston. You're right on time." She led him in.

"I know better than to be late."

She smiled. If he was forced to admit it, he'd have to say he liked Sandra better than Wife-Number-Two. She had not given in to his father's pursuit until his divorce had been final. Separated hadn't been enough. That kind of principled behavior deserved respect, even if her taste in men was questionable. She had after all married Davis P.

"Preston."

He broke away from following Sandra and headed for the person bellowing his name. "Happy Thanksgiving."

"You too." His father gestured him to sit. "Have you been back to visit Jason?"

"Yes," Preston answered, but immediately felt wary. He wasn't supposed to lay the smack down on Davis P. over beleaguering the man still in physical therapy.

"I'm getting troubling reports about his progress."

"He's working at it," Preston said, trying his best to be diplomatic. "It was a bad fall. Not something you just bounce back from. It's going to take time."

"I know." Davis agreed, seemingly. The frown he wore said there was a but coming.

"You keep asking, it puts pressure on him." Preston tried politeness again. Diplomatic. Really trying.

"It's not my intention to pressure him."

"Your intention doesn't matter. He's more worried about recovery than anyone else could ever be," Preston said. He so preferred directness. "This is his future that's on the line. Yes, it's the future of your practice too—but, worst case scenario, your patients simply find a new doctor when you retire, not someone you selected to bequeath them to."

Less diplomatic than he'd intended.

His left eye twitched twice, and then clamped shut.

"Preston?"

"It's nothing," he said quickly, rubbing the offending eye. Like that ever made it calm down.

Instinct wanted to rub cramped muscles. It just didn't work as frequently as it should.

"It doesn't look like nothing. Is this why you've been wearing the sunglasses indoors?"

"Yes," Preston grunted, and rose. "Don't worry about it. But, for the record, if it was something to worry about, after watching the way you've been driving Frist up the damned wall, I wouldn't tell you."

As soon as the words were out of his mouth his phone started to buzz. Perfect. A glance at the screen confirmed the source: St. Vincent's. All trauma surgeons called in.

Couldn't they have messaged him ninety seconds ago? It would have saved him from most of this conversation. "I have to go."

"You can't operate if your eyes are bothering you that much."

"I have drops in the car." With great effort he could open the eye now. Maybe a few minutes without Davis P.'s disapproving stare would help too.

Sandra appeared from the kitchen with a brown paper bag in hand, and followed him to the door. "Preston, take this with you."

He looked at the lunch bag. "Didn't expect me to make it through dinner, did you?"

"No." She patted his arm after he took the bag. "Practically a family tradition by now."

She was right.

"I'm sorry," he said, frowning.

She looked so surprised he almost forgot to add his thanks before he bailed. Drive slowly. One eye meant bad depth perception.

After Preston had driven out of sight of his father's house, he parked and grabbed his phone to text Dasha:

Down one eye, still want me?

His phone rang a minute later, and although her voice was muffled he could just understand her. "Come as soon as you can. Drive carefully. It's slick."

"I noticed," he said. "What happened?"

"One of those charter buses slid on bridge ice and off the railing."

"Damn."

"I'm in OR Five, join me when you can."

Courtesy of Thanksgiving, Davis P. now knew

something was up with his eyes. Would it really matter if people at the hospital knew, as well?

It could affect his probation period. Maybe they would be less willing to take a chance on the big-mouth surgeon if he was also only part time because his eyes had periods without bending to his control.

He drew a deep breath, and pulled back onto the road. As long as the drive would take, maybe his eye would clear up by the time he got there.

If not, he'd have some decisions to make.

Decision number one was easy: Drive via the route with the fewest bridges and overpasses.

And drive slowly.

Between his eye and the ice, it took Preston an hour to make what should have been a twenty-minute drive. But he made it safely.

His eye still refused to cooperate. He'd seen enough cars off the road on the way there, pumped his brake while picking through six lanes of a car obstacle course on West End to make the decision of whether to go in easy. Screw the consequences.

The parking garage was dry at least. He parked, grabbed his bag and made a dash inside to change and scrub up.

People were hurt. All hands needed on deck. He could help, even with one eye. Maybe not in a hands-on manner, only from the sidelines until it cleared up, but there was always some way to help. If he was lucky, the spasm would pass quickly and he could assist properly.

He'd risk the board finding out, and if it was considered a mark against him, so be it.

Fifteen minutes later he entered OR Five, still one eye down.

Dasha looked up when he came in, her brows lifting over the mask. She didn't comment, though. "Perfect timing. I could use an eagle eye."

Luckily, he still had one. "What do we have?"

"Perforated bowel." A tech gowned and gloved him, frowned at his eye but, like Dasha, did not comment.

He positioned himself on the other side of the table then, seeing the small body between them, glanced around the drape to see the patient. Kid. Maybe a teen. Poor girl.

Keeping his hands out of the equation, he leaned just enough to watch what Dasha did and, more importantly, what she couldn't easily see from her side, providing suggestions when his vantage point provided useful information.

Within twenty minutes his eyelids parted just enough to tell him the spasm was lessening. A few minutes later it relaxed and he opened it. "It's passed," he murmured to her.

She glanced up again then back to the patient. "Good. Help me finish with little Miss Sara here and then take your own OR. Too much need today to waste your time. Sara was the worst off, but there is still a queue of lesser life-threatening damage."

Ninety minutes later, all that remained was to close and Dasha turned to one of the nurses. "Take Dr. Monroe to a free OR and send a team with the next patient."

Preston smiled at her, hoped she could see it beneath the mask, and headed for the door, peeling off his protective gear as he went.

Flying solo. Dasha shared his screw-the-board sentiment in favor of doing right by the patients.

She could still surprise him.

And he couldn't let her down.

The locker room should have couches. Sure, there might be an on-call dorm-style sleep room, but Dasha was too tired to go there. She sat on the hard wooden bench in front of her locker, staring at the shiny sage metal. As soon as she got some energy, she'd go to the office and sleep on that couch.

Preston had the last bus crash patient in the OR, and no one needed her right now.

But if she stayed there, she might fall asleep and fall off the bench. It almost took more energy than she had to peel herself up from the bench, but she made it up and dragged herself out and toward the elevator. No stairs today, elevator.

There should be a couch in the elevator.

And the corridor.

The distance seemed shorter when she jogged or speed-walked it.

By the time she'd reached her temporary office, it took all her strength to unlock the door, cross the threshold and fling herself facedown on the couch.

"Dasha?"

A hand, large and warm, squeezed her hip and her name was repeated.

Wake up. Time to wake up.

Dasha stirred and looked over her shoulder. Preston. "Hi." Where was she? Couch. Office. "Is there a problem?"

"No. I just wanted to tell you I was out with the

last patient." He sat on the edge of the couch, a big foil-covered something in his hands.

Her stomach growled.

"Hungry?"

"I could eat the desk." She'd just been too tired to care before. A look at the clock allowed her to mark the length of her impromptu power nap. Ninety minutes of bliss.

"I have the largest turkey sandwich in history. Want half?"

"Homemade?"

"Maybe." He shrugged. "Sandra followed me to the door with it. She could have had Thanksgiving catered."

"Sandra?" Who was this Sandra? Girlfriend?

"Dad's latest wife."

"Oh." Whew. "Close enough to homemade. But for the record, I'd have taken it if you'd said it was made from out-of-date lunch meat. Gimme." She sat up, making room on the couch, and unwrapped the very large sandwich between them. Claiming the closest half, she took a bite and almost drowned in her own drool. "I don't know her, but I think I love her," she announced as soon as she'd swallowed.

"She's not bad," Preston agreed, grinning. "Probably catered, though. Picks better caterers than husbands."

"Marriage not working?"

"Seems to be working okay." He just really didn't like his father. And she understood that even better now. Dad, overachieving perfectionist, had pushed him hard. That might have been okay, but then he'd betrayed his mom. Like she herself had betrayed Preston.

Talk about something else.

"How was the last surgery?"

"Good. Don't expect any complications." Preston passed her a bottle of water, willing to share that too, it seemed. "I do wonder why they were all traveling in a chartered bus on Thanksgiving, though."

She took a drink and passed it back. "They were meeting for dinner in the middle." She was a little more awake now.

"Some kind of group dinner?"

"Reunion."

He had the sandwich at his mouth, ready to bite down, but pulled it out and asked, "That was one family?"

Dasha nodded. "Extended. Scattered over the state."

"Did we lose any?"

She held up two fingers.

"Those poor people."

She could hardly even picture having such a massive family that you'd need to hire a bus to go anywhere together, but that didn't lessen the tragedy of them losing two. All she could say for certain was that it was a horrible situation. Christmas, one month away, would be likewise ruined. Possibly forever.

"Puts my crappy Thanksgiving in perspective." Preston eyed his sandwich.

"Lots of work is much better than lots of carnage."

"Not the work." He shook his head. "I was thankful for the work. Had a small showdown with Davis P. about him pushing Jason too hard."

"Uh-oh."

"Eye flipped out in the middle. He saw."

"So he knows now?" Maybe that could be good.

"I'm not asking for his opinion or his help, get that out of your head." He read her mind. "All he knows is that something is wrong. I withheld details."

"Even if you were looking for an escape hatch, I appreciate you coming in with the eye like that," she said when she'd gotten enough sandwich in her to stop her growling stomach. "I know you don't want it known."

"It was the right thing to do."

A smile crept across her face. She really liked sharing with him, and she should try to get over that. At least until he made a decision about where they stood and whether they could be friends for real. She still couldn't contemplate being more than that…

"How long are you on duty?" he asked, finishing up his sandwich.

"Until seven."

"Twenty-four-hour rotation?"

"I don't mind. Usually it's less exhausting. Thanksgiving always involves trauma surgeries, but I've never had to call in backup before." She'd also never had such a fantastic leftover sandwich before. She took the last bite.

"Always work Turkey Day?"

She nodded.

"I guess I thought you'd spend it with the Saunderses in other years."

"Bill and Marjorie aren't from here. Always traveled home to be with family for Thanksgiving. Which he did alone this year. I'm glad he went. Sort of thought he might stay home alone and mourn some more."

That line appeared between his brows again, the partial frown that told her he was trying not to. "Mind if I stay until seven with you?"

Dasha blinked. "You wouldn't rather go to bed?"

He turned to look her in the eye, the frown line disappearing. "Oh, I want to go to bed."

The heat in his gaze and the suggestive rumble of his voice brought a happy tingle roaring to life between her legs. Maybe Thanksgiving was another time to put their past on hold.

She looked at the clock. Almost two. There were still a few hours where they could be interrupted but… She looked at the door. Unlocked. Remedy that.

Springing from the couch with more energy than she'd known she had, she locked the door and hurried back to him.

"Now?" He watched her flick off the lights and crawl into his lap.

"Yes, please. This couch is a great bed."

A slow grin lit his features and he pulled her to him. "If we get interrupted, I'm going to be disgruntled."

"Okay. I'll risk it." She leaned in and latched

on to his lower lip for a little suckle. His arms wrapped around her and his mouth opened.

Cranberry kisses… She'd have never said the taste of cranberries on the lips of your lover could be sexy. Now she doubted she would ever think of the holidays without it.

Forever changed by the silly shared sandwich with the man she loved.

Stupid. Stop thinking. Just feel, and everything would be all right.

Why would this trip to find a doctor be any different from the other trips? Nothing like a fool's errand to put Dasha into a bad mood. The other thing? The more irrational part of her mind shrieked that Preston was making her love him on purpose! Only then, when he left, would she have finished her penance.

"Tell me again why we're going to this doctor?" Dasha said, driving up I-65 toward Louisville. At least it was closer than the other cities had been.

Preston looked at her with a sharpness that rankled further. "Just because the others weren't any good does not mean this one will be crap too."

"You know, I understand you not wanting Davis P. involved, but the man has contacts. I bet you a gazillion dollars he could make a call and have someone on a plane inside seventy-two hours." Davis P.? Great, now she was picking up his bad habits.

"I'm not asking him. I don't need his help or want it."

"Do I need to draw you a calendar with a fat crayon for you to fully appreciate the rapidly approaching end of your probationary period?"

"This conversation isn't productive." Preston laid his head back.

"End of probationary period means?"

"I know what it means!"

"Do you?"

"Dasha…"

The warning in his voice wouldn't dissuade her from saying what she had been dancing around for six weeks. "If you think I'm going to let you operate without a safety net after that date, think again."

"If you think I want to operate without a safety net, think again," Preston countered, shaking his head. "Do you really think that the idea that my eyes might go wrong and I could seriously hurt or kill a patient because of it has not crossed my mind? That it doesn't keep me up at night?"

"How can I know what you think about it? You act like nothing can derail you, like you're invincible, even when you and I both know that it's happening more often."

"You want me to say it?"

"Yes. I want you to say it. Tell me how you're feeling, what you're thinking, because I can't read your mind." Well, sometimes she could, but not about this. His confidence got in the way.

"I thought I just told you. I'm afraid of hurting someone. I'm afraid of…failing a patient. Failing myself. I'm even afraid of failing you—you got me into St. Vincent's, and I know that. You might have done it because you felt like you owed me, but you still did it for me. It's for my benefit, and I appreciate that. I just…"

The anger in his voice had a purpose: it hid fear and unexpressed misery. And made her wish she hadn't pushed him.

"I'm trying to minimize the damage this can do to my career. I want this position. If I can just hold on to it until the board approves me, I wouldn't care so much that people knew about my eyes. I just don't want them messing up everything, anything…" He'd apparently reached the end of his ability to verbalize the way the worry affected him. "I'm done talking about this."

"Okay." She shouldn't try to comfort him. He wouldn't appreciate it, but she couldn't help herself. She reached over and gave his hand a squeeze, just a fleeting contact to show support, and then put it back on the wheel.

His smile was tight and swift, and he laid his head back and closed his eyes, effectively shutting himself off from her.

No, he hadn't mentioned the reason he didn't want to involve his father, but it didn't take a genius to figure it out. It had nothing to do with the board, but whatever complex emotions Preston felt about his father. However much he disliked the man or the things he'd done, he wanted Davis P.'s approval, as any son would.

Maybe the doctor in Louisville would have some answers.

A long white limo pulled up outside Dasha's cottage, clogging the small-town lane in front of her mailbox—nearly overshadowing even the trellis beside it and out-of-control wisteria she'd been foolish enough to plant and which had promptly taken over her yard. Sure, a limo fit right in.

She took a breath and looked down at herself again. It was weird to see that much fabric flowing off her body. The salon had done what she'd told them to do, and she at least didn't have her appearance to worry about. Not really. She just didn't want to go, but at least she looked the part.

Grabbing her keys, her clutch and the invitation, she exited her little cottage in the fairy-tale suburbs of Rutherford County.

The driver opened the door for her, and as gracefully as she could she gathered the yards of fabric, ducked and stepped into the limo. There was probably some secret to getting in and out gracefully that she didn't know, Preston hadn't mentioned that in his advice-giving days. Her maneuvering consisted of spinning, some more skirt moving, some clutch dropping and finally falling into the seat when she felt it at the back of her knees.

She had to make a better exit than that.

If she could pull that off, she could handle this evening just fine.

She didn't need man-candy camouflage on her arm to survive it. And she didn't need the man who'd shot down a fourth doctor there either. If none of those four doctors were acceptable to him, she had to banish the idea she'd ever be acceptable. She could love him and not need him.

But she might need a winch and a complex system of ropes and pulleys to get her back on her feet if she fell down in this ridiculous dress.

Preston sat with a clear line of sight to the entrance door in the large ballroom at the overly opulent Cumberland Resort, waiting. Dasha was never late if she could help it. She wouldn't be one of those who arrived fashionably late. She may have uninvited him, but a promise was a promise. And he would see her in a dress, by God. He might even take a picture to commemorate the event.

He glanced at his watch to be certain it was time to worry.

Five minutes late. He reached for his phone. Time to text.

Where are you?

He waited, eyes still on the door, until his phone beeped.

I'm at the winter ball.

Liar. I'm at the ball. You're not here.

I told you I didn't want you to go.

Preston smirked. Save the best of his dress zingers for in person, they probably wouldn't translate well to texts anyway. She just had to get there.

Too bad. Better hurry up before I make the hospital look bad.

I'm here…

He looked at the door again, and then did another visual sweep of the ballroom.

Cumberland Resort was renowned for its Christmas-light displays—which they began erecting in the summer and lit in the fall. Although the official holiday was still three weeks off, the ballroom glittered with so many tiny white lights that the only other light source was the small candles lit at each table.

Nice, dark and romantic…but hard to really see across the massive room by that light. He still didn't see her.

Where?

A second later a single word appeared on his phone.

Bar.

Preston looked toward the bar. No Dasha. Three women with dates, and one with dark hair. No Dasha.

What the hell was she playing at? If she'd made a fuss about going and then skipped it… He grabbed his phone again and dialed. Talking time. Text wouldn't convey his irritation properly.

The brunette at the bar answered her phone.

"Turn around," Preston said, glad the music wasn't too loud to hear over.

Deep dark mahogany hair, a strapless red dress displaying luminous skin and those breasts… Her head turned to face him, phone to her ear as she scanned the room.

"Hi," Preston said into the phone, smiling across the ballroom when her eyes landed on him.

She looked nervous. "I like your tux."

"Your hair…"

"This is the color it's supposed to be," she said,

lifting a hand to touch it. Not as confident as she'd looked a moment ago. It tugged at his heart. And his groin.

Gorgeous. Why in the world did she dye it? "It shows."

"You told me to be myself," Dasha said, smoothing her hands over the silky material, fidgeting.

Preston smiled at her across the floor, his eyes returning to hers every time someone passed between them. "I get credit for this?"

"Or blame." She smiled, tilting her head so she could look sidelong at him.

Adorable. Gorgeous. Sexy. "Don't be an idiot." He said the words like a caress. Not that it really mattered what he said. Was there any way to compliment the woman directly that she'd accept?

"You sure it doesn't look dumb?"

"Yes. Want to dance?" His first long-distance dance invitation. The first time he'd really ever wanted to offer one at the dumb old ball too.

She smiled again.

Preston hung up and crossed the floor, arm rounding her waist to sweep her away from the bar. He didn't stop until he'd found a bare spot of dance floor where they could have the illusion of privacy. "You're beautiful." He breathed the words into her ear.

She shook her head a little. Nope. Still unable to take a compliment. He wanted to kiss her.

"Why did you come?" She turned to face him, but clearly did not know what to do with her hands. He guided one to his shoulder, took the other and began to lead her in a gentle waltz.

"I wanted to."

What did she have to be so nervous about?

"I won't ask any more questions." Dasha stepped a little closer so the hand on her hip could rest instead at the small of her back. "I'm glad you came. Don't look a gift horse in the mouth, right?"

"Just call me Mr. Ed." She smelled good, and she felt better. "Don't be so stubborn next time." Suddenly, he wanted nothing more than to take her home. Peel that dress off her inch by inch. She probably had some kind of desperately sexy underwear under that gown. Garters…

She stepped a little closer, so he could feel her breath against his cheek. "You're one to talk about being stubborn." She kissed his jaw.

The song ended and another began. She made as if to step away, but he kept her anchored to him and she fell back into step with him. "Why didn't you want to come tonight?"

The face she made somehow didn't diminish her refined appearance. "Any second I'm going to do something dumb. Fall down. Eat with the wrong fork. Embarrass myself."

"Do you think everyone here is secretly pointing and laughing? There's nothing to laugh at, darlin'." Beautiful. Graceful… No matter what she'd said about not wanting to come, about not fitting in, she glowed.

"No, high-society people don't point and laugh. Well, not as grown-ups. After eighteen, no pointing and laughing allowed. Only mean talking." She was trying to joke, he could tell, but it was too close—whatever caused her to think that.

He'd failed to really know her before, but he wouldn't let these glimpses go by unexamined anymore. Whatever the future held, he'd know her if nothing else. "Did they point and laugh at you as children?"

Her nod was quick, slight and self-conscious. "Trailer-park girl in a prep school? Didn't fit in but I got a good education."

"They were idiots," he said, knowing that the words failed. He needed better words.

Still tucked against him, they swayed together, but she'd stopped making eye contact.

"Dasha." He said her name, making her look up at him again.

"If any of them are here tonight, they're jealous." He swallowed, tried again. "Not a single woman in this room can hold a candle to you. You're radiant."

Her eyes glittered but she smiled. Must have gotten the right words…or close enough. Maybe he could learn to do this.

"You want to go for a walk? The conservatories are lit up. And it's fairly warm out. We could venture outside to one of the gazebos and look at the trees."

"I don't need to be here and represent the hospital?" Dasha looked around the room, clearly tempted to escape into the safety of the gardens but not wanting to shirk responsibility.

"There's time for that. Not that anyone will notice. No one's taking attendance, Cinderella, and it's a long time until midnight." Preston spun her once and then hooked his arm around her waist again and steered her toward the exit.

They'd never done this when they'd been together. It had been a weird relationship, not that Dasha knew that. Her only real example had been a mother who'd been the other woman, and a father who had disappeared when his wife was in town. Dysfunction Junction.

What she and Preston had been seemed miles healthier. They'd gone to school together, they'd competed against each other, they'd studied together…and they'd had sex. Lots of sex. And they hadn't really talked about much of anything.

Tonight they talked. Talked about places they'd gone, where they lived, what idealized future career plans looked like. Whether the beach or the mountains was better for vacation. Everything.

Well, everything except the big issues. What might happen if his eyes couldn't be fixed? Could he forgive her? Could they be friends…give up the physical side of their relationship later?

They had an unspoken agreement to stay away from reality. Reality couldn't intercede in a wonderland of trees that glowed like tiny diamonds, where at one place a string ensemble played traditional Christmas music, and around the corner Brenda Lee was rocking around the Christmas tree.

Reality couldn't compete with indoor riverboats winding through a small indoor New Orleans, or with slow dances in an outdoor gazebo beneath stars on a crystal clear night. Thousands of twinkling lights had a way of blocking things out. Gazebo posts and rails wrapped in red velvet ribbons and greenery and the crisp scent of pine and cinnamon to complete the magic Christmas spell. One perfect night.

The problem was it all made her feel. Wrapped in an illusion of love and beauty, with this man she could not have. It made her feel, it made her want…and reality seeped back in.

Every day Dasha told herself that their unspoken arrangement would be okay just for today, one more day. Tomorrow she'd go back to being sane, break it off. No more sex. No more thinking about him all the time. No more worrying about him. Sane. And then repeated the same mental dance the next day too. It was easy to go with it. It felt good. It felt right. It wasn't right, but her body—her heart—didn't know that.

Some time late in the evening she stopped him in mid-dance. "I want to go home."

"You read my mind." He kissed the side of her neck and took her hand. They were already outside, it was only a short distance to the taxis and limos.

She stopped him before he could get far. "You can't come home with me." Time to just be honest.

The start of a scowl formed between his eyes.

"For one thing, we tend to use sex to get over feeling bad about something. That's not something I can do anymore." She took a breath. It was a night for truth. "I love you. And you deserve better than empty sex. I deserve better too. I know you want me, and I'm pretty sure I will always want you."

He started to speak and she put her hand over his mouth.

"I know you can never love me like I love you, but I won't be my mother. I won't stay in a lopsided and doomed relationship."

He moved her hand. "Dasha…"

"It's okay, Preston. I'm okay." She leaned up and pressed her lips to his. "Thank you for tonight."

"It's not okay. What happened?" He pulled her off to the side, out of the way of passersby. "Did I do something?"

"No. No, you've been wonderful. But…we've talked about everything but the one thing neither of us wants to face. What I did five years ago… no matter how I explain why I did what I did, no matter the extenuating circumstances—and I know you can understand those—the fact is I did it. The way it all came together, it was like Fate had made my future clear. One or the other, I could choose you or I could choose a career and security for myself. I chose myself, and there's no going back from that."

"Dasha."

"It doesn't matter that I love you. Not really. Because even if you think I'm good enough to move in your circles, you can never trust me. Even if you can forgive me. Not because I did what I did, but because you can never know that I won't do it again. I don't even know that. In the right circumstances I might do it again. Choose a safe life for myself and leave you to the wolves." Like if he didn't get his problem taken care of before the end of his probationary period and tried to keep going as he had been, and his pride put both their careers on the line. Dasha didn't know what she'd do.

It didn't matter that she loved him, the most loving thing to do for him might be to betray his trust.

CHAPTER TEN

PRESTON STARED AT Dasha. She'd said she loved him. She loved him, and then she'd said a bunch of other stuff about the past, not all of which had sank in. "We should go home and talk about this." When had he wanted to talk? Never. Never ever, but everything she was saying sounded very final and very wrong.

"There's nothing else to say." She kissed him again then turned away. By the time she had scurried out of sight around to the front of the hotel and the waiting limos, his shock had transformed to a sense of loss tinged with anger.

He felt the now familiar stiffening of his left upper eyelid. His eye's warning system that it was done with the world for the time being.

Preston hurried to the string of empty taxis at the rear of the line. Think about this logically.

If she loved him, she wouldn't say all that and then run away. The night had been…really pretty great. And her emotions had been dialed up since Marjorie's death.

Everyone needed love, and she undoubtedly did care about him. But she was reeling, vulnerable and mixed up. That situation would resolve itself if he stopped spending so much time with her. If she didn't really love him, it would wear off. If she did…he had to get his eyes sorted out before he could even contemplate having anything with her.

He climbed into a taxi and gave his address.

This night had gone very differently when he'd concocted the plan to meet her at the ball. That night had had a happy ending. This night…

He really had no idea where it all had gone to hell.

"Jason! Gemma!" Preston knocked louder on Jason's door. The sun was up, and so was he. Still in his tuxedo too.

Gemma answered the door. "Preston, what on earth are you doing?"

"I need to speak with Jason." He stepped around her.

"Goodness gracious, just stop and let him get to the living room. He was in bed," she chastised him, blocking his path to the living room. Even five feet nothing, she managed some natural intimidation when she squared her shoulders and poked him in the chest. "Hold your horses."

"Sorry." He resisted the urge to rub his chest where she'd been poking. Shoving his hands into his pockets, he waited for her to let him pass. She didn't until Jason had hobbled through. The leg was healing faster than the hand.

Jason eyed the rumpled formal wear. "Have fun at the prom?"

"No." He sat on the couch. "Part of it. Listen. I have a problem." Several. Start with the big one.

Preston launched into the issue with his eyes, the treatments he'd tried, the doctors he'd rejected after meeting them. "I know you can't operate yet, but do you know someone good? I really don't want to involve Davis P."

"You've been hiding this since Davidson West?"

"Yes." Should he feel guilty about that?

"Why the hell would you hide it?"

"It's a long story." Involving his father and the girl he loved breaking his heart. "And not for me to tell all of it."

"Does your father factor into it?" Jason rubbed the sleep from his eyes with his good hand. But friends didn't mind when you got them up in the early morning, right?

"Even before I saw him riding you. Has he backed off at all? I tried to tell him to dial it down." And he took his own advice and tried to dial down his own agitation.

"He has, actually." Jason pointed to his cell across the room. "Could you hand me that?"

Preston passed it over. "Please tell me you're not calling him."

"I'm calling a friend who practices in Chicago."

Preston forced himself to sit back down. "Isn't it early?"

Jason laughed. "Thought of that just now, did you?" His hair still stood at crazy angles from having just rolled from bed.

"Er, yeah."

"I'm calling his office. He'll get the message tomorrow." He stopped talking to Preston and started talking to whatever was on the other end. Voice mail? Answering service?

Gemma came in with coffee and even gave him a cup.

"Sorry about the banging, Gemma." Seemed like he spent half his time apologizing lately.

"You'll make it up to us." She eyed him and went back to the kitchen.

"What's she doing in there?" he asked Jason after he'd hung up, and made a mental note to get the woman some apples. A lot of apples. There had to be some kind of place to buy lots of apples.

"Making breakfast. She's very into the big weekend breakfast thing." Frist sure knew a lot about Gemma's habits.

"Are you two living together now?"

"Unofficially," Jason answered, and leaned back. "You going to tell me about Dasha?"

Preston leaned back in the chair and took a breath. "I'm going to try." And hope it didn't lose him his new friend. He certainly couldn't do any worse with Jason than he had with Dasha.

Monday morning arrived with a surprise for Dasha. When she arrived at the hospital, she found the office door unlocked and the lights were on. Bill was sitting at his desk.

"Good morning." Dasha smiled, glad to see him. And maybe hoping that meant she could stop acting as head of surgery.

"Morning, puddin'. I need to work, so I'm back. Getting caught up. Anything to report?"

"Uh..." Dasha sat down, glad to be on the right side of the desk again. "Had a thing with Preston, but I think he's going to be okay. He has been working really hard to get on well with everyone. Well, everyone but Nettle. He still calls him 'that cardiac a—' Let's just say he has a name for him."

"You haven't had any complaints?"

"No. Not really," Dasha said. "Jason was worried at first, but he and Preston are friends now."

"Good. I'll recommend him to the board for full privileges." Bill made a note.

"There is a problem," Dasha puffed. "He isn't going to be able to go on rotation yet."

"Something to do with the reason he called off this morning?"

"Maybe." Dasha could only hope he was going to another doctor. The other option was that he was doing something stupid that might wreck all the progress he'd made with St. Vincent's, or that what she'd said to him had made him decide not to seek treatment as proactively because she wasn't there, pushing him. "I need the morning off."

Bill gave her a knowing look.

"Don't get ahead of yourself. I'm not going to see Preston."

"Do you have any surgeries this morning?"

Did she? "Crap. Yes. One." She looked at her watch. "It should be short, though. After?"

"After," he agreed.

Preston wasn't her patient, but he was still her responsibility. She would call him, and if he didn't listen, she'd do what she had to. At least this time her betrayal would be for his benefit more than her own.

Two hours and a phone call later, Dasha found herself sitting across from one Davis P. Monroe. Preston had kept sending her call to voice mail, she'd seen him do that a number of times with the other person he didn't like to talk with: the man she now faced.

Time to come clean.

"Dr. Monroe, thank you for seeing me. There are some things you should know, starting with the day you found Preston handcuffed to the bed."

Preston got Jason into the passenger seat of his Jag and stashed the crutches behind the seats.

"Gemma's going to be mad at me forever, isn't she?" Preston looked over the top of the car to the woman Jason had fallen out of a tree for, and who now glowered mightily at him from the front door.

"She has a big heart, but she's also got a heck

of an ability to hold a grudge. So maybe." Jason waved at Gemma.

Preston got in and started the car. "You sure you're up for this?"

"I'm not the one afraid of Davis. P." Jason had also picked up Preston's method of referring to his father.

"I'm not afraid. I'm annoyed," Preston muttered, turning his phone back on. Dasha had called a few times. He considered listening to the messages but everything about her was too raw right now. Not the kind of emotional mess you wanted to make in front of your new friend. Even one effectively calling you a wuss.

"You are too. You don't want him to think badly of you, even though you go out of your way to make sure he does." Jason rolled his eyes. "You are a mess, my friend. But you're not a robot. Lose the tough attitude before we get there. We want his help."

"I'm trying." Preston dropped his phone into the cup holder and started the car.

"Try harder," Jason murmured, and leaned back in the seat, settled in for the ride.

Dasha looked over her shoulder as the door of Davis Monroe's office opened and the dynamic duo barreled in: Preston pushing Jason in a wheelchair and with a weird look in his eye. When he saw her sitting with his father, the look got less weird and more suspicious.

"What the hell are you doing here?" His words came out in a single flat tone. Not a good sign.

She stood, trying to appear calm even if she was starting to feel like she might barf on someone. She looked at Jason. No help there. A deep breath and she opened her mouth, but Davis P. was already talking.

"Dr. Hardin enlisted my help in trying to track down—"

"You told him." Preston's face went from that lovely natural tan through more shades of red than she could have accurately named.

"Yes." She had told him. And now she wanted to run away. Again.

"Because you love me so much." With those short words he made it clear to her how much he thought of that love.

This time was different from the last time. He'd understand when he'd let himself think about it, but he would not forgive her. Defending herself wouldn't matter, and it wasn't about her. It was about helping him, taking care of him, not about her image. Not about what he thought of her.

"I'm never going to be able to trust you, am I?" Preston shook his head, eyes closing for a moment.

"It doesn't matter now." Dasha reached for her bag, keeping her voice level through force of will she hadn't known she had, but the only way she'd slow her heart rate down was to get out of there. Not by running this time. She nodded to the elder Monroe and said softly, "Thank you, Dr. Monroe."

On her way past, she squeezed Jason's shoulder and did everything she could not to look at Preston. She wanted to run, she wanted to stay and fight it out, she wanted to throw up… Every emotion clouded into her overworked cranium, and she could only breathe through it. Get out with as much dignity as she could. Jason and Davis P. would have to take care of him now. Or at least try to talk sense to the prideful fool.

He had to be all right. All she could do was try to see to that.

Davis P. waited until Dasha had closed the door before he focused on his two wayward sons. Preston could concede to his father viewing Jason as a second son. He could hang with that. What he couldn't hang with was his father and the other pain-in-his-ass conspiring to manage him.

"Was that necessary?" Davis P. asked.

"Yes."

Davis P. shook his head. "She's a good woman, Preston."

"She is." Jason took the side of Dasha and Davis P. "I'm sure she just thought she was doing the best thing for you."

He wasn't wrong about this. "Neither of you know what you're talking about." Preston stepped around Jason in his wheelchair and took a seat of his own.

"She told me everything," Davis P. corrected him. "Handcuffed you to the bed so she could get the St. Vincent's fellowship. I know."

She'd told him that? And taken the blame? Preston chanced a glance at Jason, who looked suitably surprised. "It's a long story."

"You keep saying that. I'm starting to believe it," Jason murmured.

"Before you condemn the girl, there was no chance of her getting that fellowship if you'd shown up."

Preston stopped, the words shocking him to momentary silence. "You were that confident in my—?"

"No, I arranged it," Davis P. said, without a shred of shame.

Before Preston's mind cleared enough to think of something to say, his father lifted a hand to silence him. "You're a wonderful surgeon, boy, but you make bad decisions outside the OR. Like this eye business."

Preston rubbed his head, praying his eyes didn't pick up on the stress chemicals pouring through him and start to flip out. He had to get through this meeting. Dasha had betrayed his trust—which should not be a surprise—but he'd come here to do what she'd done. Sort of. "Don't talk to me about bad decisions. And right now I'm too pissed to even think about what you just said. If she told you everything, you know I need surgical intervention." Think about Dasha later. Get this over with now.

"I know who to call," Davis P. said without pause.

"You don't need to call anyone in," Preston cut in. "Jason found someone."

"Leeson, Chicago," Jason filled in. "He's flying in Thursday night, but he needs privileges. Can you clear it with the board?"

Davis P. looked between them. "Yes. I think so."

"When?"

"Today. Is there anything else you need?"

The two looked at each other and shook their heads.

"You know you could have phoned this in to me, boys," Davis P. said.

"We expected a fight," Preston admitted.

Jason shrugged. He was kind of like a turtle in showdowns with Davis P. But at least he was here, something Preston was seriously thankful for.

"I assume you want me to schedule an OR for Friday too?"

"Yes, please," Jason said, so polite.

Davis P. nodded. "I'll get right on that, then." He rounded his desk and reached for his phone.

As Preston stood and rolled Jason toward the door, his father called out, "Preston, you stay away from Dr. Hardin. Best for everyone that way."

Like he needed his father to tell him that. He'd been saying it to himself for years.

It had stopped working a couple of months ago.

Preston took off time for medical leave. Bill arranged it with the board. Other than a few early blips, he'd behaved and proved himself to both the staff and the board. When he returned, it would be without a babysitter. Dasha had done that. Or she'd helped facilitate that, and she should feel good about it and about herself. Her debt? Paid. And it should start to feel like it soon.

She finished packing up her locker and made a quick circle around the hospital to say a few goodbyes. New hospital Monday. New boss. New everything. And Preston had got the position he was always supposed to have here, at St. Vincent's. Even if Davis P. hadn't arranged it, Dasha knew in her heart that Preston was the better surgeon. He would have had the position if his father had had faith in him. St. Vincent's was the final piece of the puzzle.

She'd feel good about that part eventually. Soon would be good. Only an idiot would be sad about the inevitable. Their relationship was never meant to be lasting. She'd known that going in, known that years ago. Should know better now.

She did know better, and she should feel good about that too.

Anytime now…

Preston's knees bounced as he sat on the edge of the bed, waiting for nurses to finish dragging him through more of the pre-op drama. Or all of it, as they had failed so far to drag him through anything except changing into a hospital gown. Failed to set up the IV. Failure number one. He was keeping a list.

Davis P. poked his head in. “Do you need anything before you go in?”

Preston twisted to look at his father. “Well, a nurse who can get a line in would be good. Is your hospital peopled with idiots?” He should have had the damned procedure at *his* hospital.

Davis stepped in and lifted Preston’s hand to examine the bandage on the back. “You want me to do it?”

No. Preston’s knees bounced harder. “I want…” Dasha. He wanted Dasha there to sympathize with him about having to deal with idiots. And to smile at him when he bit back words he knew he shouldn’t be saying.

Well, he couldn’t have Dasha.

His father kept watching him, waiting calmly for an answer.

“You to do it.” He scooted back in the bed and swung his legs up.

“Maybe we can give you a little something for your nerves now too.” Just then, the nurse returned with supplies to give his intravenous line another go.

"I have to have a clear head so I can keep an eye on everyone," Preston muttered.

Davis waited for him to settle and then tied the tourniquet around his forearm. Barely a minute later he had the catheter in the vein and was busily taping it into position. "All done."

Preston looked at his hand and frowned. "Thank you." He might not get along with his father, he might think he was a jerk more than half of the time, but he could be counted on in a medical sense. He needed that for the surgery. He needed Dasha there.

"Anything else?"

"Yes," he said, pausing to make sure it was what he really wanted, "I want Dasha here."

"Is that a good idea?" Davis P. asked, sounding very fatherly. And that annoyed him too.

"Yes," Preston snapped, closing his eyes. Some time in the last couple of minutes they'd started twitching again.

"I'll see what I can do. She might be busy, though."

"Okay." He sighed. "Thank you." He paused for a moment and then added, "Dad." Maybe their relationship could change if he took the initiative. He didn't feel all that certain of it, but he could make the effort. He didn't look at Davis. If the man looked even slightly smug, he would lose the warm fuzzies he'd almost started to feel.

Davis P. entered the waiting room and sat beside Dasha. She didn't officially start work here until next week, so she had time to loiter.

"He asked for you," Davis said as he leaned back in the chair.

Dasha blinked at Davis. "Why? Does he know I'm here?"

"No. But apparently my hospital is peopled with incompetent idiots." Davis shook his head.

"You're the one who raised him," Dasha reminded him. She wouldn't take the blame for that aspect of his personality. "But what's that to do with me?"

"No idea. If you go back, take this sedative with you and see if you can get it into him. Best for everyone." He handed her the medication.

"If I go in now, he'll know I was already here." Dasha took the cartridge and looked at it longer than it took to read. She didn't rise yet. Preston was a big bloody wound still. If she went and he yelled at her, she might just bawl right there in front of all the new people she'd be working with. What an impression that would make.

"Yes. But not why. You could tell him you transferred. He'll find out eventually. Or you could just let him wonder." He leaned back, shutting off the conversation in the same fashion that Preston often did, but it afforded her a measure of privacy with her thoughts to decide.

Davis knew she loved Preston, and had been there when his son had thrown the word back at her with a double shot of derision, he knew what it would take to go in there. Even if the man could be insufferable and overbearing—and Preston was right about that—he had some good points. He didn't pressure her, at least. And he had helped with the position…

Dasha walked to Preston's room and knocked on the doorjamb.

He looked pale in the hospital gown, especially with the grim frown on his face and his eyes closed like that. "Go away."

"Okay," she said, and turned.

"Dasha."

She looked back to see him sitting up, alert with one twitchy eye. "You asked for me."

"You got here fast." He waved her inside.

She stopped at his bedside and gave the machines a long check. "I was already here."

"Why?"

"This is my new hospital. I work here now, thanks to your father's kind recommendation." She tried to hurry along this part of the conversation. "What can I do for you?"

"You left St. Vincent's?" What did the frown mean? She had no idea.

"You got custody of the hospital in the divorce," she tried to joke. It fell flat. "What did you want, Preston?"

He looked at the cartridge in her hand. "Would you observe the surgery for me? Make sure this Leeson isn't a quack?"

Dasha held up the medication. "Can I give you this so you stop making friends with the staff?"

He thought for a second and then reached his hand out, giving her access to his IV port.

"Don't you trust Jason and your father's opinions of Leeson?" She screwed it into the port on his hand and injected it. The second it hit him, she could tell. Those beautiful blue eyes took on an unfocused haze.

"I like Jason. Never seen him operate, though.

He could be a nice dude but…" He shook his head. "But…sill…inclompetent." He'd started mangling words. Be hard to call the staff names now.

"If you want me to, I will." She didn't want to. It didn't matter that she was a surgical veteran, she still had trouble stomaching even the mental image of cutting happening to the face she loved.

"Thank you." He tried to open his eyes extra-wide but his attempt to fight the drowsiness lasted milliseconds.

"Close your eyes. Stop fighting the medicine."

"Need to pay 'tention."

Attention. Good thing she spoke sedative-ese. "I'll take care of things." Maybe he didn't hate her after all. Even if they could never be together, having him not hate her made the situation the tiniest bit more palatable. Even if they couldn't ever be together, his opinion of her mattered. It had always mattered, she'd just sacrificed it in her own interests last time. Right now, it might matter a little too much…

She slipped from the room and returned to Davis P. "He wants me to observe. Can you clear it with Leeson? I need to find some scrubs and get changed."

"Will do," he said.

She ignored the warmth in her belly. It felt good to be needed, even if it was only temporary. She had best ignore it. Feelings kept interfering with her plan—the plan not to become her mother and fall for an unavailable man who would one day leave her anyway.

Hours later, the surgery over and her nerves frayed, Dasha returned to the waiting room where Davis P. sat, his hand linked with that of the woman Dasha presumed to be his wife. A couple seats away were Jason and a petite blonde.

"Everything went well." She sat between them. "Leeson will be out to speak with you in a few minutes."

"You all right, Dasha?" Jason asked. "You look a little green."

"I didn't enjoy the surgery." Strange thing for a normal person to say, but she knew they'd understand. "It was interesting. And unpleasant."

He nodded, holding up his good hand to keep her from continuing. Did he understand? Probably. He was one of the most empathetic people she'd ever known.

"My manners are faltering." Dasha nodded to the two women. "Mrs. Monroe. And you must be

Apple Butter." She smiled at the blonde, with only a little effort.

"I'm never going to live that down." The woman rolled her eyes.

"You'd think he'd have gone with Apple Brown Betty, it has a real name in it. What's your name really?"

"Gemma Holbrook."

"Nice to meet you, Gemma."

Their introductions paused when the waiting-room attendant came to her. "Dr. Hardin? Recovery nurses have phoned to ask for you to come and deal with Dr. Monroe."

"Barely out of anesthesia, and already terrorizing the staff." Dasha shook her head and followed the woman to find Preston.

His eyes were bandaged, and that should have made it easier to see him like this. She knew how much he hated a situation not to be under his control. No one in her life, except maybe her, hated being vulnerable as much as Preston did. She understood him.

"Preston?" She said his name right before she slipped her hand into his, as she would any patient who needed comfort.

Any time a procedure was performed on the

head, swelling could make the patient's appearance somewhat shocking. Even knowing that, and even though half his head was swathed in gauze, it still created an ache in her middle so sharp that her eyes watered.

"Dash. Please stay." He said the words, or some semblance of them. The drugs still made him somewhat less than coherent.

"I'll stay if you want me to." She picked up his hand, the one without the line in it, and massaged it gently. Hand massages calmed. They were lovely.

"I'm thinking," he slurred, so he couldn't be thinking too clearly, but he obviously needed to say whatever was on his mind before he could calm down and rest. "I'm not him. Okay? I'm not him."

For a second she didn't know what to say. Many levels of consciousness peeled away under general anesthesia—had he found one where he could read her chaotic mind? Or had she linked him with her father some time in the past? "I know, Preston." She rubbed his arm, just wanting him to rest. And shut up. She never liked talking to drunk or drugged people—you never knew if what they said was true.

"I'm not him," he said again, his words meandering. "Used to be." He sighed and turned his hand to grip hers. "Not now. I'm not."

"I know." She kept hold of his hand, just going with it. "You got better." What else was she supposed to say?

"Okay." He laid his head back again, swallowed and breathed, "So…don't…don't…" His thoughts stuck on that word for a few more repetitions before he'd organized some other ones. "Don't…not love me…anymore."

Her throat constricted. Don't pay attention to what he says, no matter how hard that is. She took a breath. "Everything is okay."

"Say it," he demanded, as much as a groggy man could demand anything.

"You need to rest. Don't get all worked up." She deepened the massage, her thumbs working at the palm, stroking the muscles. "I'll stay so no one incompetent messes anything up."

"Me. Me. I messed up."

Don't listen. It was akin to believing a fall-down drunk saying he loved you. Drugs made people do and say things they normally would never say. Just comfort him and let him go back to sleep.

"You didn't mess anything up." She shifted her

attention to the back of his hand and stroked him. It seemed to calm him a little.

"Don't not love me anymore," he said again, with better clarity.

She nodded.

He couldn't see her nodding. She tried again. "Okay." The word came out in a whisper, but she got it out before he had to say the words again. Before she had to hear the words again.

Dasha stayed by Preston's bed, holding his hand to keep him relaxed until Leeson released him from Recovery. In the bustle to move him to his outpatient room, she escaped.

And now, evening, she found herself summoned again. He really needed to stop calling her. And she really needed to stop jumping up and running to his side when he did call her.

Dasha knocked on the carved white door to Preston's apartment.

A minute later she heard movement inside. Another minute and the door swung open. There he stood with his bandaged head and eyes.

"Is there no one here to take care of you?" She looked around him, not seeing anyone about.

"No," he answered, sounding tired. "Want the job?"

"Not funny." She stayed out in the hall. "What do you need? Besides a babysitter."

"I need to talk to you." He stood back, making the invitation plain.

Dumb idea. Really dumb idea. She sighed. "Fine."

"You could fake some enthusiasm." He shut the door behind her and locked it.

"I don't fake it." She left him to follow. It was his home, and he had been getting around on his own before she'd arrived. The couch looked comfy. She sat.

Not at all what she expected his place to look like. The building had once been some kind of business, the upstairs probably some sort of factory or maybe an office. The wall that faced the street consisted of a large swath of massive, multipaned windows. Bright light from the streetlights shone in, and no doubt it would be even brighter during the day. Probably painfully bright, given the state of his eyes. The heavy fabrics and abundance of wood offset the windows a little, but it still looked kind of like a hunting lodge and a modern bachelor pad had had a baby. A baby that might smoke cigars.

"How are you?" he asked, bringing her focus

back to the man. Like she'd not been aware of his every move while she'd tried to ignore him. He hovered in the seating area but didn't sit.

"I'm fine," she said.

His head turned in the direction of her voice, and he reached out to locate her on the couch before sitting beside her. "I thought this would be easier if I didn't have to look you in the eye at the same time. I was wrong. I don't know what you're thinking."

"I'm wondering why you summoned me." And maybe what she'd done recently that demanded a heavy conversation.

"Summoned?" Preston queried, frowning. "Invited."

"Okay. Invited." Go with it. Get the whole messy business over with.

"I thought you'd be at the hospital when I got out of Recovery." He sounded too alert—like he hadn't taken his pain medicine.

Did he remember Recovery? That was probably the thing he didn't want to see in her eyes, the things he'd said.

"I mean, I hoped you'd be there after Recovery," he said a few seconds later, when she'd failed to speak.

"I didn't think it would be a good idea. And, honestly, I know you don't really want to hear this or care about any of it right now, but it's hard for me to see you." Especially like this.

"It's hard not to see you," he murmured. "And I care."

"Well, then, let me off the hook. Why am I here?" And who did she have to hurt for leaving him alone in this state?

"I told you earlier. I don't want you to…well, I didn't say it very well, but I still meant it," he said the words softly. "I don't want you to stop loving me because I'm an idiot."

He remembered what he'd said in Recovery. Dasha didn't know what to say, what to think… She hadn't prepared for this possible outcome. She couldn't let herself think that he loved her. He didn't even want to be her friend, he'd said. He didn't forgive her, at least he'd never said he did. That was important.

"Dash?"

"Huh?"

"I'm not him." He sat stiffly, not moving his head much, no more than was needed to talk. It hurt. She could hear it in his voice.

"Yes. You said that before," Dasha said slowly, then took a slow breath. "Who are you not?"

"My father."

Not *his* father. Good. Though she still wasn't putting it together. "I know you're not him."

"But when we were together before, I was. I was just like him." He managed to find her hand, and held it, which was when she noticed the tremble in his usually steady hands.

"Don't do that to yourself." She liked knowing where a conversation would go before she got fully invested in it, but right now she had no clue. He wanted her to love him, okay, she did, but she wouldn't let him take on a burden he hadn't earned. "You weren't like him."

"I was. I was shallow and self-absorbed. To the extent that you could never talk to me about your past. I didn't even know that your parents were dead or gone. I didn't know anything personal about your life outside school. I was just like him. Our relationship was about how you made me feel, and I only focused on the good parts. I didn't want to know the bad stuff because it might mess with the way I felt about you."

"I could have told you…"

"I should have asked. I should have shown an interest. You showed an interest in me, in my family, all that."

"Yes, but I was..." She stopped and started over. "You can't take the blame for my behavior. And if you had asked me, I would have probably lied. I didn't want anyone at school to know who I was. I didn't want people to pity me. I thought I could be this whole different person, ignore all the bad parts of my life. If no one knew about them, maybe they could just not exist for me anymore. None of that was your doing."

"You think no one knew you didn't come from money?" He laughed a little, but stopped quickly. It hurt. "You suck at lying, Dash. I should have known you then. Really known you."

"It's okay. I don't blame you." She shook his hand a little, trying to redirect his attention. "Have you taken your pain medicine?"

"Stop. I have to say this. You want my forgiveness. You have it."

She shifted, uncomfortable, and inexplicably scared.

"Dasha."

"Thank you..." She whispered the only words that came to mind.

"I forgive you. If I'd been a better man, you would've never felt like you had to do what you did. If you could've talked to me...your reason for wanting the fellowship was much better. You deserved it. And if you hadn't…derailed me going to the interview, I would have gotten the position. Davis P…my father had arranged it. But you deserved that fellowship."

She tried to say something, but her throat had closed to so narrow a passage that even if she'd had words, they couldn't have gotten through. All that came was a strangled attempt, and agitated bouncing of one knee.

"Please say something."

"I…" No words. Still no words, at least not any of the sort that wouldn't shriek her unworthiness.

"Oh, hell." He reached up and started picking loose the tape holding his dressing over his eyes.

"Preston!" She leaped from the seat, her hands flying to pull his hands away from his eyes. "Stop that. That tissue is very fragile. Dr. Leeson wants the bandages on until he sees you tomorrow."

He tugged his hands free of hers and latched on to her hips. The next second she was in his lap and his arms were around her.

"Are you taking the pain medication?"

"Yes." His arms anchored her to him.

"Poor puppy." She whispered his name and as he rested the curve of his forehead on her shoulder, she gave in and wrapped her arms around his shoulders. "You need to rest."

"Can't."

"Yes, you can. We'll settle you in the recliner." Why did every man she knew have one of those?

His slow, deep breathing might have led her to believe him sleeping if he had not only just spoken. "I never forgot your scent." His arms tightened. Her chest tightened.

"I never forgot the way it felt to be in your arms. To kiss you. The sounds you make when it feels just right…"

She bit her lips to hold them together, to hold *it* together.

"I thought of you every day. When life got too rough, I slept. I could always find you in my dreams." His arms unwound and his hands slid up, not stopping until he had both her cheeks, his thumbs stroking away tears she couldn't hold back. "I don't want to only hold you in my dreams."

She still couldn't manage to think, let alone say anything.

"Please don't cry."

"What do you want to happen? What do you want with me?" Finally a thought. It would have been harder to look in his eyes. It would have meant he could see how much she wanted this to be real, to see how much she wanted him. But at the same time she desperately wanted to see his—to know he felt.

"Wedding," he said simply, and smiled.

"Do you love me?"

"Am I being hard to understand?"

"You have to say it. You have to mean it."

"You flourished at St. Vincent's. Everyone there loves you." He kept her from squirming away from him. "I love you, Dasha. Do you understand? I love you. I forgive you. Forgive me…"

"Are you sure?"

"Do I sound uncertain?"

"I'm not sure I'm not hallucinating." She whimpered.

"I'm the one on drugs." He laughed and then groaned. "Laughing hurts."

"So stop. Just say it again." She wound her hands around his wrists, needing to hold on to him, needing to be grounded when he said it again.

"I love you. I want to marry you. I can forget if you can. I promise to keep you too busy making new good memories to give a half of a damn about the past and our mistakes."

She nodded. He couldn't see her, but his hands on her cheeks caught the desperate motion.

"A fine time for you to learn how to be quiet."

She laughed. "I know. My timing is terrible."

"There's the voice I want to spend decades whispering in my ear."

"Don't forget this later." She kissed his hands and stood. "You need to rest, but if you take all this back when you've sobered up, I will—"

"I know, I know." He stood at her urging. "It's a good thing you aren't ever going to need to accept any more proposals. You suck at it."

"I'm better at propositions." She led him to the recliner and made him sit. "When is your next dose of medicine due?"

"About an hour ago."

"You said you took it!"

"I did, seven hours ago. I wanted to make sense when we spoke."

Dasha groaned and went prowling to find the medicine. "What am I going to do with you?"

She already knew the answer: Take care of the fool.

Then marry him.

* * * * *

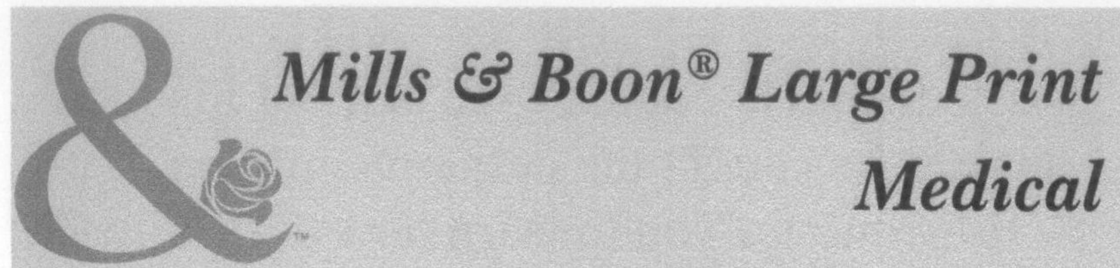

October

200 HARLEY STREET: SURGEON IN A TUX	Carol Marinelli
200 HARLEY STREET: GIRL FROM THE RED CARPET	Scarlet Wilson
FLIRTING WITH THE SOCIALITE DOC	Melanie Milburne
HIS DIAMOND LIKE NO OTHER	Lucy Clark
THE LAST TEMPTATION OF DR DALTON	Robin Gianna
RESISTING HER REBEL HERO	Lucy Ryder

November

200 HARLEY STREET: THE PROUD ITALIAN	Alison Roberts
200 HARLEY STREET: AMERICAN SURGEON IN LONDON	Lynne Marshall
A MOTHER'S SECRET	Scarlet Wilson
RETURN OF DR MAGUIRE	Judy Campbell
SAVING HIS LITTLE MIRACLE	Jennifer Taylor
HEATHERDALE'S SHY NURSE	Abigail Gordon

December

200 HARLEY STREET: THE SOLDIER PRINCE	Kate Hardy
200 HARLEY STREET: THE ENIGMATIC SURGEON	Annie Claydon
A FATHER FOR HER BABY	Sue MacKay
THE MIDWIFE'S SON	Sue MacKay
BACK IN HER HUSBAND'S ARMS	Susanne Hampton
WEDDING AT SUNDAY CREEK	Leah Martyn

0914 LP 2P P1 Medical

January

200 HARLEY STREET: THE SHAMELESS MAVERICK	Louisa George
200 HARLEY STREET: THE TORTURED HERO	Amy Andrews
A HOME FOR THE HOT-SHOT DOC	Dianne Drake
A DOCTOR'S CONFESSION	Dianne Drake
THE ACCIDENTAL DADDY	Meredith Webber
PREGNANT WITH THE SOLDIER'S SON	Amy Ruttan

February

TEMPTED BY HER BOSS	Scarlet Wilson
HIS GIRL FROM NOWHERE	Tina Beckett
FALLING FOR DR DIMITRIOU	Anne Fraser
RETURN OF DR IRRESISTIBLE	Amalie Berlin
DARING TO DATE HER BOSS	Joanna Neil
A DOCTOR TO HEAL HER HEART	Annie Claydon

March

A SECRET SHARED...	Marion Lennox
FLIRTING WITH THE DOC OF HER DREAMS	Janice Lynn
THE DOCTOR WHO MADE HER LOVE AGAIN	Susan Carlisle
THE MAVERICK WHO RULED HER HEART	Susan Carlisle
AFTER ONE FORBIDDEN NIGHT...	Amber McKenzie
DR PERFECT ON HER DOORSTEP	Lucy Clark

0914 LP 2P P2 Medical